Stories for Lilah

Stories and Poems

Inge Logenburg Kyler

authorHOUSE®

AuthorHouse™
1663 Liberty Drive
Bloomington, IN 47403
www.authorhouse.com
Phone: 1 (800) 839-8640

Text and illustrations by author.

Published by AuthorHouse 05/12/2015

ISBN: 978-1-5049-0855-9 (sc)
ISBN: 978-1-5049-0854-2 (e)

Library of Congress Control Number: 2015906322

Print information available on the last page.

This book is printed on acid-free paper.

Dedicated not only to Lilah Rose Dickerson,
but to all persons young at heart!

Contents

Donald, the Ornery Goose

Donald and Daisy Goose lived on an island. It was a beautiful island with tall green trees and shiny green bushes surrounded by a cold clear mountain stream that bubbled and gurgled over rocks and stones.

Donald and Daisy were very happy. Donald was a big white goose with an orange bill. Daisy was smaller. She was a gray goose with an orange bill like Donald's.

Donald was very proud and protective of Daisy. In fact, he was so protective that he wouldn't let any other goose be on the island. If a duck or goose tried to come near, Donald would chase it away.

Daisy watched Donald honk and hiss at people who went by. "Oh Donald," she would say, "you are such a brave goose," and she looked at him with lovelorn eyes. And yet although Daisy thought Donald was very brave and handsome, she missed not being able to visit with other geese or ducks, because he chased them all away.

"Donald," she timidly said one day, "maybe you shouldn't be so hard on others when they come to visit,"

"But Daisy," Donald said, "you know that when we build a nest for our family, you will want to be left alone. You'll be busy with the children and won't have time to visit anyway."

That was true, thought Daisy, but just the same, she would like to visit now and then with someone besides Donald. One day when she saw some old friends that she hadn't seen in awhile swimming towards the island, she asked Donald, "please, can we let them stay?"

"All right," said Donald. He would do anything for Daisy to make her happy. He stood back and watched their old friends, Harold and Virginia, as they climbed up the bank to the island. They all had such a nice visit and Donald tried hard, after that, to remember what Daisy said, not to scare everyone away.

But sometimes Donald forgets. If you should go to a place where you see a goose wandering around, don't go near it! It might be forgetful like Donald and try to chase you!

~

Nordic the Worm

Nordic had a headache, and the day had just begun.
He longed to leave his dwelling, and he longed to feel the sun
But yesterday his mamma told him that he must stay in
For robins had flown back to town. And true, he'd heard their din.
She told him of the saying, what the early bird could get,*
And of young boys with fishing poles. He hadn't seen THEM yet.
He curled up in his burrow, but it seemed so damp and cold.
He wondered of the great outdoors, and thought he would be bold….
Although his mamma warned him, he decided to go out
And slithered to the doorway, when he heard a loud voice shout:
"I see one! Bring a shovel!" And he knew his doom was near.
Quite fearful now, he tunneled deep, his life seemed, oh so dear!
And as he tunneled deeper, he thought never would he doubt
Again his mamma's warning, when she says "Do Not Go Out!"

*There's an old saying that says "The early bird gets the worm!"

~

The Cricket That Wanted to See Snow

Leaves were falling everywhere, one, two, three. Sometimes a bunch fell at one time, and soon the ground was covered with them.

"Why are the leaves falling?" asked the littlest cricket. "What is happening?"

"It's fall," said mamma cricket. "In the fall the leaves come off the trees, and in the spring the trees get new leaves."

"What happens in between?" asked little cricket.

"In between fall and spring is winter, when snow starts to fall," said mamma cricket.

Little cricket thought about the snow. He wondered what it looked like and what it felt like.

One day the wind started blowing. It got colder and colder. Little cricket's mom told him that soon they would need to burrow underground where they would be safe and warm.

"But, Mom," protested little cricket, "I want to see the snow!" His mom tried to explain that snow was cold and that no crickets or grasshoppers could survive the cold days of winter if they stayed above ground.

Little cricket wasn't convinced. He decided to talk with Mr. Finch about snow and winter. Mr. Finch was busy pulling the last of the sunflower seeds out of a garden.

"Indeed," said Mr. Finch while cracking open a seed, "snow can be dangerous for many creatures, even though it can be quite lovely to see." He then went on and explained that snow was almost like starlight falling from the sky. When it lands on trees and bushes, it turns everything white. When the sun shines on snow, it sparkles and looks quite nice.

"When it snows," said Mr. Finch, "everything gets really quiet, unless the wind happens to be blowing. If the wind blows, some of us have to huddle in pine trees to stay warm and hunker down until things quiet down.

"Also," continued Mr. Finch, "when it snows everything gets very cold, so cold, that the ground becomes frozen and is hard to walk on. We finches don't even like to sing when it gets that cold. The wind stings ours eyes. Even pools of water freeze and it is hard to find something to drink."

Little cricket listened carefully.

"Well, Mom," he said, "I think I have heard enough. Maybe I don't really need to see snow, but it is nice to know what it is!" Mamma cricket smiled. Together she and little cricket burrowed deep down underground. As soon as they were snug in their little house underground, the last golden leaves fell to the ground and white snowflakes started covering leaves, trees, and everything in sight.

~

Another Chair at the Table

Henry Brownbridge was unhappy for he just received the news:
"You're going to have a playmate! If you could, what would you choose?"
His mother seemed excited, so he didn't want to say
He really was quite happy with the way things were today!

"A brother or a sister? Well," his friend said, then went on
"My little sister cries a lot and wakes me up at dawn,
And mother doesn't have the time for games with me, these days.
I have to keep an eye on little sister when she plays!"

Now Henry felt much worse with this. He dragged his feet along.
"I wonder if they'll still want ME! Maybe I won't belong."
He sat beneath a big shade tree and felt depressed and blue.
He liked his life the way it was. "Now what am I to do?"

But then his dad took him aside and said, "Son, don't feel sad.
You'll be the bigger brother and for that you should be glad!"
The role of bigger brother really didn't sound that bad.
"Okay!" said Henry as they walked, "I'm glad you are my dad!"

Some people look the same, that's true, but there is only one of you!

The Bear That Lived in the Park

Bennie the black bear lived in a park. He didn't know it was a park. All he knew was that it was home. Bennie loved the thick forests of tall pines, hemlock, cedar and birch trees. He also loved the grassy open places where he could roll in the colorful wildflowers.

Bennie especially loved the big old trees and he loved digging for ants and termites in old stumps that were scattered throughout the forest. He loved the little creek that wound through the park. He was sure to find all kinds of fish, and they tasted, oh, so good!

But most of all, Bennie loved the camping season, as that was when People came to the park and brought all kinds of foods. He could smell the food as soon as they set up camps or started serving food for a picnic.

It didn't take long for Bennie to realize that people were not neat with their food. He found scraps of food all over the campground and all through the park.

"Don't," said Mother Bear, "get into the habit of eating people food. It will make you sick, but worse than that, it could lead you to Big Trouble!"

Bennie didn't tell his mother that he had already tasted people food, and that he really liked it. It wasn't as if he went searching for it. Yet, maybe in a way, he did, because whenever he smelled People, he followed the scent until, sure enough, there they were, and right in front of him was the food!

Bennie especially liked scraps of peanut butter sandwiches and French fries. Oh, how good they tasted!

Bennie soon learned that if he came out of the woods just as people started setting up their picnic lunches, they would take off running. Then, the table was all his! This was SO easy!

He also discovered that backpacks left by a tree or tent contained all kinds of candy bars, sandwiches, and beef jerky. It was easy to rip into the packs and get the good stuff!

"Where are you going, Bennie?" asked Mother Bear just as Bennie was starting to go down a path.

"Oh," said Bennie. "I'm going to check something out."

"Remember what I told you," called his mother as she watched him disappear into the woods.

"This is easy," thought Bennie to himself as he headed for a table where People were just starting to set out food from a big picnic basket.

"BEAR!" yelled a little boy, and everyone scattered out of the way.

"Hey," yelled a park ranger who just happened to be nearby, posting bulletins that read: *Please do not feed the bears!*

"There's that pesky bear," he said as he called for help on his radio. Bennie had already started digging into the food. In a minute another park ranger came rushing up to help. "Get him," yelled the little boy and his family hiding behind a tree.

ZAP went the tranquilizer gun that one of the park rangers fired towards Bennie! Bennie looked up in surprise as he felt something sting him and he suddenly fell over in a heap. "Oh no," he thought before he passed out. "They got me!" He then fell into a big sleep.

The park rangers loaded him into the back of a truck and drove out of the park. They drove and drove and drove. Finally they pulled over and carefully opened the cage they had put Bennie in, and opened the door.

Bennie stumbled out and looked around. This wasn't home. This was unfamiliar woods. He shook himself and then ambled into the forest.

"Maybe mom was right," he said to himself. "Maybe this is the Big Trouble she was telling me about. I should have listened to her. I didn't even get to say goodbye."

Meanwhile, Bennie's mother realized he was missing and went out to search for him. She sniffed and sniffed the trail for a long time and walked and walked until she finally found him. Bennie was so glad to see his mom that he said, "I promise I will never go near people food ever again." And you know something? He never did!

~

So, when YOU go to the park: Never feed the bears! Never leave food out where bears can find it, and remember to leave the park nice and clean!

~

Buzzie the Teddy Bear

Buzzie the Bear had come to town,
Had come to town to stay,
For he was packed tight in a box
And came from far away.
The box was ripped, its side was torn
But he was safe inside,
And though he bounced from side to side
He still survived the ride.
He traveled on to grandma's house.
She found him at her door
And was surprised to see him
When she came home from the store.
He helps her roll out cookies
As he sits upon a chair.
Just maybe you have seen him?
Buzzie, the teddy bear!

~

Heading South

"Run for your life," squawked Claretta Goose just as Mr. Jones came driving down to the pond in his golf cart with lights blazing and horn blowing. It was night time. Claretta Goose and her family had just settled down by the pond in Mr. Jones's front yard when she saw Mr. Jones coming straight towards the goose families that had gathered for the night.

"Run, run!" echoed Lucy and Lacey Goose as they, too, gathered their families and started running for cover. "Head to the woods," yelled Daddy Goose as he hurried along while trying to help other goose families get out of the way.

It had started out being a very nice day. Claretta Goose and her family and friends had so enjoyed their day at the pond. The weather had warmed up and the young goslings had a great time practicing their swimming strokes. But now Mr. Jones was after them. "Get away from my pond," Mr. Jones yelled as he chased them with his cart.

Claretta Goose didn't want to leave. She felt safe away from the fox and coyote that lived in the woods, but she had no choice. She had to quickly move her family!

"Mom, mom," sobbed Jimmy and Johnny Goose together. "Why is Mr. Jones being so mean?" They were running hard, trying to keep up with their mother. "Well, Dears," Claretta Goose tried to explain, "It's hard to understand humans sometimes. But we have to do what they tell us."

Finally all of the little families were herded into the dark woods at the edge of Mr. Jones's yard. Once the youngsters got over their fright, they settled down close to their parents for their evening lessons.

Claretta Goose felt lessons were very important. There was so much to teach her offspring before they grew up and flew away. They were almost ready now to go off on their own. They had grown much in a short time.

"Our lesson tonight is about roads," began Claretta Goose. "What's a road, Mom?" asked Jimmy Goose. "The road," said Claretta Goose, "is that patch of ground that is packed down hard by dirt or gravel where people drive noisy vehicles all hours of the day and night."

"Oh," said Clarissa Goose, who always caught on quickly. "Those big things that have flashing lights and are noisy are vehicles?"

"Yes," said Claretta Goose. "Vehicles won't stop if they see you in the road. It is your job to move out of the way."

"Don't vehicles ever go to sleep?" asked Johnny Goose who was getting a little sleepy. "No," said Daddy Goose, "they don't go to sleep. They are on the roads day and night." Clarissa was getting bored and asked, "When do we start our Big Journey South?"

"Oh," said Claretta Goose. "It won't be long now. We have to wait for Daniel Tree Frog to give us the signal to leave. He is our friend and watches out for us."

"Tomorrow," announced Daddy Goose, "we will begin our flying lessons." Sure enough, the next day when the children were all gathered in a safe area away from Mr. Jones, they learned how to use their wings and feet to get up in the air, how to soar, and how to land. Johnny and Jimmy Goose were so excited that they ended up having several crash landings!

One night when the big orange full moon rose high in the night-time sky, a strange noise echoed through the meadows and woods.

"That's Daniel Tree Frog," said Claretta Goose. "He is letting us know that we must begin our Long Journey South." By now the children were nearly as big as their parents. They were excited about this new adventure.

"When," asked the Goose children altogether, "can we start our journey?" "Next week," said Daddy Goose, and sure enough when next week came, there was not even one goose left on Mr. Jones's lawn.

~

Baggie's Christmas

Baggie Badger loved the meadow where he found a perfect home.
He felt it was a "keeper." No longer need he roam.
He chased off all the neighbors with a growl quite fierce and loud.
He liked his own seclusion, and he didn't like a crowd.

That is, until one Christmas, when his den seemed, oh, so bare.
He wished, while he was walking that he had a friend to care.
One day it was Coyote who saw tears in Baggie's eyes.
"Well Baggie," he suggested, "how about if you and I

go share a Christmas dinner. Do come over to my place!
It sure would be my pleasure if you then could say Grace."
So Baggie, ever after was more careful with his "roar."
He made friends and wasn't lonely in the meadow anymore.

~

Aaron, The Ambitious Mouse

Aaron was an ambitious mouse. That meant he had lots of energy and big ideas. He wanted to do many things. But what he wanted to do more than anything else in the world was to type a letter to Priscilla. Now this was back in the olden days when people used machines called typewriters to write letters. Aaron had seen them and had watched people use them in the office room where he lived. If he could type a letter to Priscilla then she would think he was much smarter than some of her other boyfriends.

After much searching around, Aaron finally found a typewriter that didn't have a cover on it. But when he found one, he found out he couldn't push the keys down because he wasn't strong enough. What to do?

While he sat down to do some thinking, the door of the office opened and a large gentleman with a curly red beard walked in. A man with a bald head followed him. "Now then," said the red-bearded man, "I want a typewriter that works like this one," as he pointed to a big typewriter on a desk, "only I want it small enough to fit in my daughter's doll house. I want to surprise my daughter Tami on her birthday. She loves her little doll house and has a little office room in it. I thought a typewriter would look really nice in it. Never mind the cost. Just send it over to my house when you finish it." Then the red-bearded man left. Note: A typewriter was a machine that had keys almost like an iPad.

The little bald-headed man looked at the typewriter and frowned, mumbling something about "making a typewriter small enough for a doll house." Before he left the room, Aaron jumped in his pocket and went along.

The little bald-headed man lived in a house full of tiny things that were just right for doll houses. Aaron was excited as he watched him start building a tiny typewriter.

When it was done, the man wrapped it in a little box and put it in his coat pocket. Aaron jumped in his coat pocket before he closed the door.

When the bald-headed man went to Tami's house, Aaron jumped out of his pocket and hid underneath the television set. Sure enough, little Tami was delighted with her typewriter and was happy to put it in her doll house that included many other things that really did work.

When night came, Aaron found a piece of paper and began typing a love note to Priscilla. When he was done, he found his way back to the office where he knew he would find Priscilla. She was so excited over the love note that she agreed to marry him right away. Aaron took Priscilla over to Tami's house where they set up house keeping in the little doll house where they lived happily ever after.

~

Dear
Priscilla

East is East and West is West

"I just don't get it," Katie said, holding her hand against her head.
"Why do we need to learn this stuff? I think I've really had enough!"
She shook her head and stomped her feet before returning to her seat.

"Directions really aren't that bad," said Ted, a skinny little lad.
"The sun, you see, sinks in the WEST when it is time for us to rest,
And pops up in the East each day while we go off to school or play.

And North is where the cold winds blow. At least that's what my dad says so.
While SOUTH is where the robins go in winter when it starts to snow."
But Kate was unconvinced that she could figure out how this could be

Until one night she went to bed when the sun was sinking, very red.
"That's WEST!" she yelled, "it has to be! I now know directions!
Lucky for me!"

~

Jenny Goose Gets to Lead

"It's time," said Jenny's mom, "that we prepare for our journey." "But why?" asked Jenny, looking around at the shimmering gold poplar leaves on the trees by the river. "Everything is so beautiful," she went on. "I want to stay here!"

Jenny's mom looked at her and said, "Things will change soon when the cold winds from the North come down and the river will freeze solid." Jenny wasn't sure she knew what freeze meant, as this was her first year with changing seasons. Just then her dad flew in and sat down with them. "I've talked to everyone," he said, "and we agreed to hold our first session tomorrow at 8 o'clock a.m."

"Why so soon?" asked Jenny and her mom together. "Well," said her dad, "we've been watching the clouds and have been feeling a cold wind. We need to get going before we get trapped inland by the winds."

Jenny knew it was useless to argue with her dad. He was pretty much the leader of their little flock. Everyone followed his instructions.

It was still early morning and a layer of thick fog hung over the pond. It was so thick you couldn't see the trees in the woods. As Jenny stood on the bank, other geese started flying in and landing with a big skid, whoosh and splash! One after another they glided in, until there were at least a dozen or more geese, all making a lot of noise with their clacking, clicking and honking!

Jenny was happy to see some friends she hadn't seen since spring. There were Clarissa, Tom, John and Henrietta. Tim, Lisa, Mary and Marlin were there, too. They all chattered excitedly until finally Jenny's dad gave a loud HONK that meant everyone needed to pay attention and listen.

Together they flapped their wings and struggled to get into a V formation. "It takes practice," said her dad, "to fly properly, but you will learn quickly. You will also learn how to be a leader."

"Oh no," said Jenny. She wasn't sure she wanted to be a leader. Just then she heard her dad say, "Jenny, you are flying much too low and too far behind. You need to keep ahead with everyone else." It took awhile, but soon Jenny could keep up with everyone else. She also learned what the word "draft" meant. Draft is the whiff of air that a flying goose creates like a road in the sky, that geese behind can follow. She found she could almost glide with hardly any effort, and soon felt comfortable with this new idea of flying.

"We will take turns leading," said her dad, "because it is stressful to be a leader for a whole trip. Jenny," he went on to say, "we'll see whether or not you can lead. Since this is your first trip, I'm not sure whether or not you can."

The whole clan of geese gathered for a quick nap. A full moon rose over the trees. Suddenly Jenny woke up just in time to hear her dad say, "This is it, everyone. Let's get going." Jenny felt very grownup, being part of the flight group. "Don't worry," said her friend, Micky, "you will feel the magic of it all pretty soon." Soon they were soaring higher and higher until they were far away from what had been their summer home.

Micky was right. Jenny was feeling really excited. She stayed in the line where her dad told her to go, as they soared over the pond. One by one they changed places in line as they each took turns leading the group. Soon it was her turn, and she headed to the front. "Whew," said Willie Goose. "I was starting to get tired, so I am glad you are here." Jenny took the lead. It was as if a magnet was pulling her. She felt happy and excited.

But she was relieved when she felt dad goose beside her. "Good job, Jenny. Now you fall back and let me lead the rest of the way. Maybe tomorrow you will get another chance to lead, as we have quite a way to go." Jenny fell back in line with the others. "I did it," she thought to herself. "I actually got to lead!" And that was Jenny's first experience with flying south with her family and friends!

~

Kite Time

Although the wind still bites my nose, and
Grandma says she nearly froze,
I know it's spring, for friends of mine are flying kites.
It's outdoor time!

~

The Festival of the Bugs

Harold, the Praying Mantis, loved night time, as it meant he could catch bugs quite easily for a good meal. That's when bugs flew around the bright lights that people had by their doors and patios.

There was just one trouble with lights, that was the fact that they attracted other Praying Mantises, and sometimes Harold didn't get along with them, especially the Queen Praying Mantis because she would catch other Mantises and bite off their heads! The fact that she was much larger than the rest of the Mantises meant that she was easy to see.

Harold loved swirling and whirling around the evening light bulbs. It was great adventure as well as good feeding time.

One fall evening Harold flew to Mrs. Apple's house where there seemed to be a lot of commotion. "What's going on?" Harold asked one of his friends. "Tonight," said his friend, "is the End of Summer Festival, when all the insects of the outdoors gather to participate in contests and games."

"What fun," said Harold. "Count me in!"

That evening Harold enjoyed participating in the great festival when everyone he knew was swirling and whirling around the big porch at Mrs. Apple's house. Of course, he was careful to watch out for the Queen Praying Mantis, but he didn't see her around. That night he also enjoyed visiting with the other Praying Mantises, as this was a special festival of friendship. So remember, when you see a lot of bugs around a light at the end of summer, that means they are celebrating the End of Summer Festival!

~

There's a Robin On My Lawn!

A woodpecker is pecking, pecking, pecking holes up in a tree.
A flock of geese is soaring, sailing, swiftly screeching over me.
A mourning dove is cooing, wooing, calling, bawling in the weeds.
The wind is breaking, flacking, baking, shaking, planting little seeds.
Grasses are curling, swirling, leaning, getting greener day by day.
Buds are big and bulky, budging leaves to come in May.
Tulips are growing, showing blossoms that will soon be reddened blooms.
In the forests far from cities, wild things climb from winter rooms.
And my toes are itching, twitching, yearning, burning to be free
Eager for the summer waters, puddles, pebbles, that's for me!

Playmate

Billy Joe was my best friend, but fusses, grumbles, argues so!
I get so mad at Billy Joe!
He can't play fair, he can't play right, and all the time he likes to fight!
I wonder where he is tonight?

~

Turtle Finds a Friend

Muddy Turtle lived in the murky bottom of South Lake. He liked his lake home because he was seldom bothered. By that I mean Muddy Turtle liked to be left alone. Sometimes Rocky Turtle would ask him to go with him here or there, but Muddy always said no.

Sandy Fish tried to be friends with him, but Muddy turned her away. "Come on, Muddy," Sandy Fish would say, "let's go explore the north bank together."

"No," said Muddy. "I have something else to do." Muddy didn't really have anything else to do, but he didn't want Sandy Fish or anyone else, for that matter, to know that.

In fact, Muddy was rather a lonely turtle. He would swim around the lake bottom and bob up for air and bugs, and sometimes he felt just plain miserable.

He didn't know why he felt that way, but when somebody came around and asked him to come along, he felt even more miserable when he turned them away.

"No," he said to Willie Bass. "I don't have time." Willie Bass had asked him to go with him to the little lake at the end of South Lake.

One day, Ellie Eel came by and said, "Come along with me, Muddy. We can explore the lily bed." But Muddy said no and started to turn away when suddenly he heard Ellie Eel starting to cry. "What's wrong, Ellie?" he asked as big tears were rolling down Ellie's face.

"I've asked everyone in the lake and no one wants to be my friend," Ellie sobbed. Muddy Turtle looked at Ellie and thought to himself that he didn't know that someone else might be feeling as lonely as he did. This was a new thought!

"Ellie," Muddy Turtle said in a quiet voice, "don't cry. I'll go to the lily bed with you."

"You will? Oh Muddy, you've made me so happy!"

Muddy Turtle and Ellie Eel swam along to the lily bed. Muddy had to admit to himself that it felt good to have a friend beside him. He also enjoyed seeing all the water lilies in the lily bed. From that day on he decided that whenever someone asked him to come along, he would go. After all, maybe by his being a friend to someone else, that would make two people happy....himself and someone else! That was a good thought. Muddy Turtle didn't feel miserable anymore after that.

~

What If?

What if carrots grew on trees and wild horses swam in seas?
What if all the grass was pink and dinosaurs were not extinct?
What if teeth were blue, not white, and crows could moo or baa in flight?
What if doors swing up, not in, and all the roads were made of tin?
What if snow fell up, not down, and bears lived everywhere in town?
What if bicycles had skates, and all you had to eat were dates?
What if water that you drink came from a bush, and not a sink?
And what if elbows and your knees would
whistle every time you sneezed?
And here's the big one, are you ready? Instead
of you, you could be Smeddie?
And every time you crawled in bed, you slept not flat but on your head?
What if all these things were true? I'd run and hide! Well, wouldn't you?

~

A Can in the Pond

Ribby Green Frog was disgusted. “Someone,” he said, “has thrown garbage in my pond!” Ribby had dived down to the bottom of the pond just as a pop can plopped on a giant water lily. “Wow,” said Ribby. “I could have been killed.” He looked at the can and tried to push it off the water lily, but it wouldn’t budge.

“What will I do now?” he stuttered. “I guess I will have to have my party somewhere else.” Ribby Green Frog had been planning a spring party and had told everyone to meet at the big water lily. But how could they meet there when a big pop can is on the top of it!

“What’s the matter, Ribby,” asked Bobbie Bluegill who was just swimming by. “Some dumb human went and threw another pop can in our pond,” said Ribby, “right where I was planning to have a party.”

“Oh,” said Bobbie Bluegill. “I see what you mean,” she said while looking up at the pop can that just about squashed the beautiful big water lily.

“What can we do about such things,” asked Ribby, feeling quite down. “Well,” said Bobbie Bluegill, “maybe we can get someone to help. Maybe your friends Bimmie and Bummie Raccoon could come up with a solution.”

Ribby thought about that. That evening when Bimmie and Bummie Raccoon came down to the pond for a drink of water, Bobbie told them about the problem.

“I know,” said Bimmie and Bummie together. “Let’s drag a trash can from neighbor John’s house. If we set it by the pond, maybe humans will use it for their pop cans instead of dumping them here in the pond.”

That night when neighbor John was sound asleep, Bimmie and Bummie Raccoon rolled his back yard trash can down to the pond. Neighbor John didn’t miss it until a couple of days later when he happened to walk down to the pond and saw his trash can right by a big rock. “Well I’ll be,” he said. As he started to move the trash can back to his yard, he stopped when he noticed there were several pop cans on the bottom. “Humm,” he said to himself, “maybe I’ll just leave it down here and get myself another one.”

And that’s how a trash can ended up by the pond. As for the party that Ribby wanted to have by the big water lily, he was able to have it after all because Bimmie and Bummie were helpful in moving the pop can off of the lily. Of course the real reason they agreed to move it was that they had hoped there would be something left in the can for them!

~

Rutherford P. Bear – Looking for a Home

My name is Rutherford P. Bear, and I've been everywhere.
I hear that is uncommon for a brown and fuzzy bear.
I did not let my color and I did not let my size
Keep me from going forward to explore the seas or skies,
For I've seen the shores of Ireland, and I've seen the China Wall.
Just name a land or country! You can bet I've seen them all!
But now I want to settle and I'm looking for a home.
A bear gets mighty lonely when he always has to roam.
There's something I should tell you: it might sound a little strange
That I'm TERRIFIED of babies, and I hope that I can find
A home where kids are older, for I think they'll be more KIND!
So maybe you will see me, sitting on a shelf or chair
And if you do, remember: I am Rutherford P. Bear!

~

The Boy Who Turned Into a Dog!

"Why should I have to listen to them?" Joey said to himself. Just because he had taken a candy bar from a candy stand, his mother made him do special chores and grounded him for a week. He also had to pay back the people for the candy.

"I'll fix them. I'll leave home. Then they'll be sorry." Joey jammed some clothes into a little red suitcase and slammed the door as he headed outdoors. He started for town, and walked beside some old unused railroad tracks. The tracks were lined with elderberry and dewberry bushes. He plucked some of the black juicy dewberries and popped them into his mouth. He was just getting ready to pick some more when a voice suddenly yelled, "Stop!"

"Who said that?" asked Joey and he looked around anxiously. No one was there. "I must be hearing things," he said to himself as he reached for another berry.

"Don't you ever listen? I said stop! When you pick my berries, you are stealing!"

Joey drew his hand back real quick and looked all around. All he could see were more berry bushes, high brush, and a little white fluffy cloud that seemed to hang low.

The little cloud suddenly took on a shape as it said, "Yes, it's me, Cloud, and those are my berries you are eating!"

"Clouds don't eat berries!" Joey laughed as he reached for another berry. "You don't like to listen, do you?" said Little Cloud. "I'm not really a cloud, but this is the form the Great Angel gave me so I can watch over you."

"Watch over me?" said Joey. "That's silly."

"Maybe you think so, but I have great powers and if you don't like to listen to people, I can turn you into a dog," said Little Cloud as he swooped down lower and lower.

"A dog?" Joey stepped back and started laughing. He laughed and laughed and popped berries into his mouth in between his laughs. Suddenly he started feeling very strange and felt something heavy behind him. It was a tail!

"What's going on …?" but before he could say anything else, he felt himself shrinking until his clothes popped off and fur appeared all over his body. He was, indeed, a dog! He opened his mouth to say something but all he could say was, "woof!"

"There!" said Little Cloud. "You were too sassy for your own good. Until you act better and learn how to respect your elders, you will be a dog!" Little Cloud floated off above the trees.

"Woof! Woof," barked Joey. He could not talk. He could not carry his suitcase. He suddenly had four feet, or rather, paws! "Oh well," he thought to himself, "this can't last. Maybe I ate too many berries and this is just a bad dream." With that, he headed for home.

Just as he reached his back porch, he heard crying. It was his mom crying and crying. His dad was standing by and had his arms around her.

"Now, Dear," he said, "don't blame yourself. He'll come home. Wait and see." Just then his dad saw him and said, "darn stray dog! I don't need you hanging around here," and he picked up a rock and threw it at him. Joey ducked just in time. "Hey," he tried to shout, but all that came out was "woof!"

That night Joey shivered and tried to stay warm under a bush. He was also hungry. He ran around to the kitchen door and looked in through the glass. His mom and dad were eating dinner. They were eating fried chicken, his favorite, and mashed potatoes and gravy.

"Woof," barked Joey, sure they would give him a piece of chicken. "Woof yourself," said his dad and he threw a glass of cold water on him.

Joey did not like having to stay outside all night. Everything looked dark and spooky. He saw a police car pull into the driveway. Were they looking for him? He wondered if he could change back into a boy if he could get into the house. But just as he got to the back door, his dad came out and threw cold water on him again.

"Scram, straggly dog," he said, and Joey scampered off to the bushes. All night he huddled in the bushes, trying to keep warm. He found half of a candy bar that someone had tossed away, and gulped it down.

The next morning he ran down to the railroad tracks. Maybe he could find Little Cloud. But there was no sign of him. Feeling sad, he ran back to his house. He saw a car pull up and his Cousin Jimmy got out of it. "Jimmy," he heard his dad say, "we are happy you can stay with us until we find Joey." Jimmy looked quite happy. While Joey hid in the bushes, he saw Jimmy ride Joey's new red bike that his dad had given him for his birthday. Then he saw his friends come by and they were all playing with Joey's toys. He tried to snuggle up to them, but Jimmy chased him away with a stick.

"That does it!" thought Joey, and with his tail between his legs, he headed back to the railroad tracks. "I'll just stay here and maybe Little Cloud will come back." He started feeling sorry for being rude to his parents. "Oh, I wish I could go back home! I so miss my mom and dad!" and he started to whine, like dogs do when they are sad.

Just then Little Cloud appeared. "Joey," he said, "if you are truly sorry and promise to be better, you can be a boy again. But you have to promise that you will try harder to behave and be good! Also, no more stealing!"

Joey looked up at Little Cloud with watery eyes. "Oh, I promise! I promise! I just want to go home!" He looked up to see Little Cloud disappear back into the sky, and felt himself changing back into his old self. Quickly, he ran home.

"Mom, Mom," he yelled, as he ran up to the door of his home and saw his mom on the porch. "Oh, Mom, I love you so much!" he said as he threw his arms around her and sobbed, and she hugged him back. From then on, he really did try to be good, and every time he saw a stray dog, he tried to be kind to it.

~

The Little Spaceship That Got Lost

Marybeth and Bridget were playing with their dolls in the grass by a little lake. Marybeth and her parents were staying in a cottage for a week, and Bridget had been invited to come along.

"I'm glad you came, Bridget," said Marybeth. "I get lonely when I am all by myself." They bundled up their dolls with blankets and started to walk along a little path around the lake.

"This lake is called Forgotten Lake," said Marybeth, "because hardly anyone knows it's here." Both girls found some flat stones and skipped them across the lake. Suddenly, a strange noise and a big puff of smoke came from around the bend. "What was that?" asked Bridget, and they both cautiously ran to look.

"Wow!" said Marybeth. "Do you see that? What is it?" A shiny flat sauce- shaped disk was leaning against a big old apple tree. As they watched, they heard a voice say, "let me out! Let me out! Please help!" The door on the top of the disk was wedged against the tree.

"What should we do?" asked Bridget. "Let's see if we can help," said Marybeth. Very quietly and carefully they crept up to the disk. It looked harmless, and when they took the courage to touch it, it felt cold.

"Let me out! Let me out!" called the voice again. With both hands, the girls shoved and pushed until the door of the disk popped open. A little person dressed in bright blue jumped out. "Where am I?" the little person asked as he rubbed his head.

"You're near Forgotten Lake here on Earth," said Marybeth. "Who are you and where are you from?" asked Bridget. "I'm Arne from Magnum I," said the little person.

"Well," said Bridget, "we've never heard of Magnum I! Why are you here?" Both girls weren't sure whether to be scared or not, but they certainly were curious.

"If this is Earth," said Arne, "then I am truly lost. Oh dear! Oh dear! How will I ever get home! Dad told me not to touch anything or start pressing buttons until he got home from work, but, well, it was my birthday and I just couldn't wait to try out my birthday present." Arne looked like he was ready to cry.

"This is your birthday present?" asked Bridget. "How cool is that! But if you are from another planet, how come you talk and look like us?"

"Did you expect that I would be a freak?" asked Arne. "I remember dad telling me that Earth people think that anyone living on another planet must be a freak! Oh, how will I ever get home?" By now Arne was sobbing and sobbing.

"Don't cry, Arne," said Marybeth. "I'll go and get my dad. He'll know what to do!" As Marybeth ran to get her father, Bridget stayed behind to keep Arne company. "Dad," said Marybeth when she found him in his workshop. "I need your help really bad."

"Oh?" asked her dad, "and what might that be?" Marybeth told him about Arne and how he needed to get home. "A spaceship, eh?" He wasn't sure if Marybeth was making that up or not, but he followed her back to where she had found Arne and the little ship. "Dad," said Marybeth, "this is Arne." Arne looked at her dad through his tears, and said "do you think you can help me?"

"Humm," said Marybeth's dad as he looked over the buttons and dials on the space ship. "I don't see a HOME button, but I have an idea. Let's see if I can build a little tower and send a signal to your folks. Maybe they will be able to come to your rescue," and he hurried back to the workshop to start building. All night he worked on wires and coils and pieces of plastic until finally he had completed building a strange looking antenna. As he started pulling wires this way and that, he finally was able to send an S.O.S. signal through space.

"Brum, brum, hum, boom," went the signal while sparks and lights flew in all directions.

"I don't think they hear it," said Arne and he started to cry again, getting tears running onto the peanut butter sandwich that Marybeth and Bridget had made for him. Finally he curled up on the porch chair and fell asleep. Marybeth and Bridget curled up in blankets beside him. In the middle of the night Marybeth sensed a bright light and lots of commotion. "Arne, Bridget, dad, mom! I hear something down by the lake." They all rushed out of the house, down the bank until they saw an immense shiny spaceship resting on the grass at the edge of the forest.

"Dad," yelled Arne as a big person came out of the spaceship and walked toward him. "Well, Arne, I hope you realize that if it had not been for the signals that we received, you might never have made it back home again," said his dad, while hugging him.

"Oh, Dad, I'm sorry I didn't listen," sobbed Arne. "But I'm glad you found me!"

"Thank you! Thank you for watching over my little boy!" called Arne's dad as he swooped Arne up into his arms. He tucked both Arne and the little spaceship into the big ship. Marybeth's family watched as the big spaceship shimmered and shook and then with a mighty whoosh, soared up into the sky and disappeared into space!

~

The Dodo

There was once a bird, a dodo
Who lived very far away.
A very strange and large bird,
He is not around today.
He lived close to Madagascar
On an Indian Ocean Isle.
His life was not so lengthy
For he lived but for awhile.
He was fat, and he was awkward
And he fell as easy prey.
People came, ate him for dinner!
There are no dodos today!

~

The Mushrooms That Aren't

"But why, Grandpa?" asked Mitt. "Why do we have to do this?" Mitt was upset over having to help clean up around the campground.

"Grandson, you ask why? Why does the sun rise in the east and set in the west? Why do you have to eat breakfast or go to bed at night..." said his grandpa as he pulled out some rakes and wastebaskets.

"Oh, I get it," said Mitt. "It sounds like another of your 'that's the way it is' sayings! You got me! I'll do it! But I won't like it," Mutt muttered under his breath.

"We can't always like what we have to do," said his grandpa, "plus, as you know, when we work and do things, it makes everything around us look nice. You should feel proud that people don't know we are around. We are special."

"Yeah, yeah. I know! I know! People gave up believing in us elves long before I was born!" said Mitt, not convinced that he was important and necessary to get things done. I haven't forgotten the story about my long gone cousin Will who was hit by an auto crank back in the days of Henry Ford and his Model T when people had to use an auto crank to start a car engine."

"Well," said his grandpa. "I hope you remember he was hit because he forgot Rule I for all elves. Rule I means that we should: always work quietly so people won't see you."

"What did happen exactly," asked Mitt.

"Well," said his grandpa, "your cousin Will forgot Rule I and thought it would be great fun to scare a little girl. The little girl screamed, and her father dropped the crank right on top of your cousin Will."

"What happened then," asked Mitt, although he had heard the story many times.

"As I have told you before, we elves disappear if one of us gets hurt or even killed. That's where that saying comes from "here one minute and gone the next.'"

"But," asked Mitt, "if he disappeared, how does anyone know anything really happened?"

"It was the clover," said his grandpa. "When an elf gets hurt or dies, a green clover plant pops up in the grass. But also remember that people see the clover plant but they cannot see the elf. Now we really must get busy as it is our job to clean this place up before people come back tomorrow."

"Why don't people clean up things themselves?" grumbled Mitt. His grandpa responded with "it's kind of sad, but people just never learn how to clean up after themselves. That's why we elves are so important."

"Who do people think cleans everything? Well, maybe they are just plain dumb!"

"I have to agree," said his grandpa. "People don't seem to have a clue how we take care of everything." With that, Mitt and other elves got together to busy themselves cleaning the campground. When they were done, they put their tools away. Very silently they turned into mushrooms.

So if you see mushrooms around the campground, they just might be elves in their daytime disguise. Of course not every mushroom is an elf, but only an elf knows which ones are and which ones aren't.

~

Rule I: Don't go around scaring people!!

Red Winged Blackbird

The red-winged blackbird comes in spring. I see him land on everything,
In meadows, marshes, field and town
Where green replaces all the brown
Of brittle stalks of winter's sting.
Oh, how I love to hear him sing!

~

Sign of May

I know for certain when it's May, that's when the wrens begin to play
Their noisy games up in a tree
Trilling songs quite joyfully! Trilling, maybe, just for me?

~

Chipmunk

With a rustle and quick footsteps, and a flash of tiny tail,
Little chipmunk comes a'begging at the campsite, without fail!
Some potatoes and some melon, and a hunk of bread or two,
And if you try not to scare him, he might do a trick for you!

~

When Every Day Was Christmas

"I wish Christmas was every day," said Johnny. He had just finished opening all of his presents. The house looked so cheerful with the decorated tree, the strands of holly berries and greenery draped over pictures and hallways. He also loved the stacks of cookies, candies and other special treats. All of that made the house smell really good.

"You would get tired of it every day," said his mom, not even looking up from her crocheting project. "No," said Johnny, hugging his Rutherford P. Bear. "I wouldn't."

The next morning after he had just awakened, he was startled by a strange noise. It almost sounded like Santa Claus. How could that be? Christmas was over. Quietly, Johnny tiptoed out to the living room. Sure enough, there was the Christmas tree looking just like it did Christmas Day, with presents piled here and there.

"Wow!" said Johnny, "another day of Christmas! How lucky can I get?" He played happily with his new toys even though some of them were the same things he had received the day before, including Rutherford P. Bear, which meant he now had two bears!

The third morning he slept in just a little, but when he went downstairs, there again was the Christmas tree and lots of presents, including a third Rutherford P. Bear!

"Another bear! Whew! I am one lucky person." That night, after stacking all of his new toys in a corner, he crawled into bed with all three Rutherford P. Bears.

But on the fourth morning when his mom called him to get up, he couldn't. He had eaten so many cookies and so much candy that he had a stomachache.

"Come Johnny," his mom called. "It's Christmas and there are presents for you to open."

"I don't feel so good," said Johnny as he pulled the covers up over his head. He heard his mom come up the stairs. She put a bunch of presents in his room and handed him a fourth Rutherford P. Bear.

"Four bears? Where will I put another bear," he asked as he looked at the three bears already in his bed.

On the fifth morning, Johnny still wasn't feeling well, but he dragged himself downstairs and saw, oh, no, another Rutherford P. Bear sitting under a brightly decorated Christmas tree! His dad was sitting at his desk, going over bills. His mom came in with a plate of cookies but Johnny noticed she looked awfully tired! By this time, Johnny was starting to lose interest in the whole thing. Not only that, he noticed that his mom and dad had started quarreling.

"Stop it!" he yelled!

"Johnny, wake up! You're having a nightmare," he heard his mom say.

He looked up. His mom, with a concerned look on her face, was standing beside his bed. Beside him, Rutherford P. Bear was tangled up in blankets. There were no other bears in his bed.

"Oh Mom, I guess maybe it's a good thing that Christmas comes just once a year, he said as he hugged his one and only Rutherford P. Bear. His mom and dad didn't say anything. They just both bent over and gave him a big kiss!

~

The Friend Who Moved Away

Where is my friend who skates with me, to laugh, to run, to climb a tree?
Where is my friend? I want to play, and build a fort with him today.
Oh yes, that's right. He moved away!

~

The Rock in the Woods

Once upon a time there was a rock that looked forward to getting bigger. He noticed that he had been getting bigger, as time went on, but he really wanted to be a boulder. A boulder is a great big rock. Little Rock was hoping that eventually he, too, would be a Big Boulder.

Little Rock soaked in the hot sun and enjoyed the coolness of the rain and evenings. Snows came and went. Years went by. The Earth rumbled around him as time went on. "I'll be a Boulder soon," thought Little Rock to himself. He proudly noted that he had gotten bigger than what he had been before.

Little redstarts flew in and sat on him. The red tailed hawk circled over and landed to play with a meadow mouse on his broadening ledge. White daisies bloomed and faded out beside him. The red Indian Paintbrush leaned against his broadening base.

"Soon, soon, I will be a Big Boulder," he said to himself just as a seagull perched on him. "Why do you want to be big?" asked the seagull.

"Oh, to be big and strong would be so grand! Everyone would admire me and would be jealous that I was so big," said Little Rock who was getting bigger every day.

"Well," said the seagull, shaking his head wisely. "I have traveled all over the world and I have seen what happens to big boulders."

"What? What happens to them?" asked Little Rock, now very curious.

"I have seen that the Big Boulders are not happy at all," said seagull.

"But why? Why are they not happy to be big and strong?" asked Little Rock. "Tell me!"

"Well," said seagull reluctantly, "I have seen Big Boulders splattered with dreadful colors of paint, which makes them look dreadful. The paint doesn't seem to wear off, so they are scarred for life. Sometimes there are awful words written on them, too. No, some of the Big Boulders that I have seen, are not as happy as you, Little Rock."

Little Rock thought about what the seagull said and he became very sad. Little Rock grew bigger and bigger as days went by, and he began to worry more and more.

"Why are you so sad?" asked seagull on one of his returning trips.

"I fear the paint and the writings that you told me about," said Little Rock. "I know there is probably nothing I can do about it."

The seagull was quiet for awhile and then he said, "Little Rock, I think I can help you. I'll carry a seed from a fir tree and plant it by you. When the tree gets big, it will protect you forever. And so it was. As Little Rock grew, so did the little fir tree that seagull planted. Soon Little Rock became a Boulder, and he was a very handsome boulder. But the most handsome thing about him was the large fir tree that towered and sheltered him from the bright sun. So if you are in the woods and you see a fir tree growing close to a big rock or boulder, you will know those are two special friends taking care of each other.

~

My Brother

My brother's always building toys. He thinks he's super smart!
Although I must admit that he can draw a nifty chart
as well as making things that move or fly, which can be pretty cool
but I just wish he'd play with ME! when he comes home from school!

~

Maude Mouse and her Flower Garden

It all began when Maude Mouse visited Tresa Chipmunk and saw the lovely flowers that grew around Tresa's house close to the woods. "Oh, such beautiful flowers!" said Maude.

"Yes," said Tresa, "and they are all mine. But you can pick some, if you like."

Maude was so impressed with the flower beds that she decided to try to grow some, too. Maude's house was hid beneath a mound of straw in the middle of a vacant lot that had a For Sale sign on it. First, she decided to draw a design on paper to show just what flowers should go where. Then she took her shovel and started digging and getting the soil ready. Next, she took her little straw basket and went around to gather seeds from flowers that she saw growing here and there.

Maude found two lily-of-the-valley sprigs in Mrs. Brown's flower garden. She also managed to dig up two small cosmo plants and one marigold plant. She took these home and soaked them in some water. While they were soaking she went to Mrs. Clay's house and found three four o'clock seeds, two clumps of discarded iris bulbs and even a dahlia bulb that Mrs. Clay had forgotten to plant.

All the rest of that day, Maude was busy planting. She was so excited that she could hardly wait to see things grow and bloom! Each day she carefully watered her flower bed. She was so busy that she didn't notice the children that came to play ball, or the men who came and looked at the For Sale sign and said, "this is a fine place for an apartment building." Rains came. The sun shone. Soon the lot was blooming with different shades of flowers of pink, yellow, white and blue.

Children came and picked bouquets of flowers for their mothers. Their mothers came to see where the flowers came from. They were surprised to see the vacant lot full of flowers blooming everywhere. How angry the mothers became when they heard that an apartment was soon to be built right where all the flowers were growing.

Several mothers got together, picked a flower bouquet and went to the Town Hall to protest the construction of a building on that vacant lot. Newspaper men and photographers came and took pictures of the mothers in the flower garden. Pictures of Maude's flower garden were soon appearing in the newspapers and on television. People started getting upset. "Why," they started asking, "should a building be built on this lovely lot? This would make a fine park for the children, too. We don't need an apartment building!"

Mr. Mayor came out and looked at the flower garden. He didn't want to make the mothers mad. Nor did he want any of them to throw a pie in his face if he didn't listen to them. He also wanted to get re-elected as he liked being Mr. Mayor.

When the people in the community brought in a petition asking that the vacant lot be saved from being built on, Mr. Mayor presented it to the City Council. Not everyone wanted to save the lot from being built on, but Mr. Mayor stood his ground. A vote was taken. The City Council rejected the proposal to build on the lot. Instead, garden clubs started planting more and more flowers on the lot. Flower bouquets were picked and taken to hospital rooms. People smiled as they walked past the now beautiful lot. People came from miles around to see it. No one ever knew that the flowerbeds were all from Maude Mouse's idea. As for Maude Mouse? Well, she couldn't be happier!

~

Ivan, the Gecko

"Ivan," called his mom from the bottom of an old scrub oak tree. "Come back here right now!" Ivan was having a good time, and didn't want to go back.

"Ah, Mom, he said, "I'm just playing by Mr. Glenn's garage."

"No, no, Ivan," exclaimed his mom. "Mr. Glenn's garage is no place for a gecko."

Ivan liked playing in the garage. He especially liked hiding from Mrs. Glenn and then popping up now and then to make her scream.

"Now!" repeated Ivan's mom, and Ivan reluctantly turned around and headed for his home in the oak tree rock bed.

There wasn't much for him to do at home. He was too little, said his mom, to be able to do anything other than really boring chores. At least Ivan thought they were boring!

On his way home, Ivan heard a deep raspy voice, "Hi kid," said the voice.

"Who are you?" asked Ivan, as he spun around and looked up to see a pair of squinty eyes looking down at him.

"I'm Edgar Skink," said the voice, still looking down at Ivan.

Ivan had never seen a skink before. He felt small and scared.

"You lookin' for adventure?" asked Edgar Skink.

"Well," started Ivan, "I was having some fun until my mom called me to come home, and that's where I'm heading now." Ivan held his head down as he talked to Edgar. It made him uncomfortable to be near a lizard so much bigger than himself, for he could tell by looking at Edgar's feet, that he was a very big lizard. He could feel Edgar's eyes staring down at him.

"We can have some adventure before you go home, kid," said Edgar. Ivan wasn't sure what to do. He didn't want to get in trouble with his mom, but he didn't want to offend Edgar, either.

"Well," Ivan stammered. "What kind of adventure were you thinking of?" He still didn't have the nerve to look up at Edgar. When finally he did, he saw that Edgar's eyes were narrow and slanted, whereas his own eyes were round and beady.

"How did you get such strange eyes?" asked Ivan before he realized that maybe that was a rude question to ask and now he might really be in trouble. He hoped Edgar wouldn't pick up his big feet and stomp on him!

But instead, Edgar laughed. Ivan was relieved that he was taking it so well.

"Oh yes, my eyes are different than yours," said Edgar, laughing. "That's because I'm me and you are you! We certainly wouldn't all want to look alike!"

"Now," said Edgar, "follow me!"

Ivan whipped around again and followed Edgar as he started jumping towards Mr. Glenn's garage. Ivan knew his mom wanted him to come home, but he was curious to see what Edgar had in mind.

Just then, the garage door flew open! Ivan heard some noise and looked around just in time to see Mrs. Glenn bearing down on them in her jeep.

"Run, quick!" yelled Ivan, very scared, but Edgar wasn't paying any attention. Edgar was standing in the middle of the garage waving his head up and down while Mrs. Glenn was starting to drive her jeep into the garage.

Ivan quickly backed out of the garage and covered his eyes. He heard a loud scream from Mrs. Glenn as she stepped out of the jeep. Edgar started running towards her! Mrs. Glenn picked up a broom and swung it at him! In the confusion, the garage door started coming down and just missed catching Edgar's tale. Edgar rolled over three times as he tumbled out of the way of the garage door as it slammed down with a loud "KER BANG!"

"Now," said Edgar as he brushed himself off, "wasn't that fun?"

"Maybe you think that was fun, but we both nearly got killed," said Ivan as he started running for home.

From that day on, Ivan stayed away from Mr. Glenn's garage. Anyway, he found it was just as much fun to scare Mrs. Glenn when she was sunning by the pool. At least that wasn't so dangerous!

As for Edgar Skink, well, when Ivan saw him a few days later, he noticed that part of his tail was missing. He was going to say something to him, but thought better of it. Anyway, his mom was calling him. She had just baked a blackberry tart from all the berries that were growing down in the field. THAT was something Ivan could not pass up!

~

The Beet Garden

Once there was a little elf whose job it was to take care of a beet garden. He was very proud of his beets and at the end of the summer he would pick them, and store them away for the winter.

A sly fox watched little elf one summer and thought what a tasty meal he would make. One morning he perched at the end of the garden and waited for little elf to come by. But the little elf was very clever, and sensing danger, stayed in his home in the tree where he could look down and see the red fox waiting for him.

The fox waited all day and finally gave up and crept away. Little elf came out of hiding and tended to his garden. The moon was very bright and gave a lot of light that made it easy for little elf to hoe and weed.

The fox happened to go by the beet garden later on his way home and seeing the little elf, thought again what a tasty meal he would make. "Now I will get him," he said aloud.

But little elf had not raised his beet garden just for food. It was also his protection. As the sly fox made a leap for him, little elf jumped into a beet leaf, and the fox, to his surprise, found himself falling, falling, falling into a deep dark pit beneath the cluster of beet leaves!

The fox pleaded and pleaded for little elf to help him out of the hole. After he promised that he would never try to harm him again, little elf threw down some twine that he pulled off a climbing bean pole, and freed fox. The fox kept his promise, and little elf went back to tending his garden.

~

The Covered Bridge

Alvin always knew when it was Sunday, for on those days Sunday Pastor Butler drove by his home bright and early. Alvin saw Pastor Butler many times but only on Sundays did he drive by in his silver car so early in the day.

But this Sunday something seemed wrong, for Pastor Butler parked his vehicle by the side of the driveway near the old Covered Bridge and walked over to pat its beams. "What a shame," he said, "that you are to be torn down."

"Torn down?" said Alvin out loud, although no one except other forest animals could hear him. Alvin, you see, was a very bushy-tailed brown squirrel. He had been sitting on top of the bridge while cracking a hickory nut when he heard Pastor Butler speak.

"Why would anyone want to tear down this friendly old bridge?" said Alvin to no one in particular.

Pastor Butler walked back and forth a few times and finally said, "maybe there is a way to save you, old friend," and he got into his car and went on his way.

Alvin had a miserable Sunday. He kept thinking how awful it would be to see the fine old Covered Bridge torn down. That evening, when all the little occupants of the bridge gathered for their usual Sunday picnic, Alvin told them what he had heard.

Mr. and Mrs. Sparrow were very upset at the news. Tillie Spider nearly fell off the high beam in the bridge when she heard about it. Edgar and Ellen Wasp became very quiet and sad. "What will we do?" they all asked. "We just can't let anyone tear down this dear old home!"

"But, but, what, can we do?" asked Lily Frog who lived under the bridge. While they were quiet in thought, the wind blew warm, and the branches from the maple trees along the riverbank brushed against the old worn Covered Bridge timbers. The last rays of evening sun cast long shadows across the old planked bridge floor.

Mr. Sparrow was the first one to speak. "We must let people know how important this old bridge is," he said. "If we work together maybe we can come up with a plan." When he finished talking, all the Covered Bridge creatures huddled together in thought. Finally they came up with a plan they decided to try right away.

The next day when Mr. and Mrs. Peters drove up to the bridge, Mrs. Peters said, "Henry, do you hear those songbirds? I have never heard them sing so sweetly before." They rolled down the windows of the car and listened as the little sparrows sang their melodious songs. "Such a beautiful bridge," said Mrs. Peters, and Mr. Peters agreed that it was, indeed, a very fine bridge. They parked their car and got out to walk around it.

"Oh look at all those lacy spider webs," said Mrs. Peters as they peered up at the high beams.

Just then Mr. and Mrs. Brown drove up in their truck. Mr. Brown was one of the city council members who had given his approval to tear the bridge down. "Oh, listen, Fred, do you hear the little sparrows singing?" Mrs. Brown asked as she rolled her window down and listened to the song birds and watched them twitter and flitter around the bridge beams.

"Eh, dear?" said Mr. Brown, getting red in the face. "It's just an old bridge, Martha, we need to tear it down."

"But why, Fred?" asked Mrs. Brown. "It has such charm. Maybe we could use it for a foot path and build another bridge on down the river."

"Martha, Martha," said Mr. Brown shaking his head, "that would cost more money than the township has. It's too expensive to keep up an old bridge."

"Well, then, we will just have to find a way to raise some money," said Mrs. Brown, as they drove off in their shiny red truck.

That evening Mrs. Brown and Mrs. Peters started calling all the ladies in the community and told them about the old Covered Bridge and how they would like to save it. Together they talked of ways to raise money. "I can start baking those cherry pies everyone likes," said Mrs. Brown and we could start a "Save the Bridge" fund. "Good idea," agreed Mrs. Peters. "I can start making dried flower baskets to sell." Soon all the ladies started thinking up ways to raise money to save the bridge.

That Tuesday night at the Town Council Meeting, all the ladies filled the council chambers by their presence and demanded that the Council vote to save the bridge. "If we have enough sales over the next year," said one of the ladies, "we could set up a special fund to use for preserving and taking care of that beautiful old Covered Bridge.

The council members listened to the ladies. They weren't sure that would work, but finally they gave in and decided to save the old Covered Bridge only, they said, "if enough money is raised. Maybe we could build a nice little park beside it for people to use as a picnic area."

Thus it was, that the bridge was saved for a park area and another bridge was built on down the river for vehicles to use. When the little park area was completed beside the old Covered Bridge, the bridge creatures held a big party to celebrate. "We did it," they all said together, but you and I know that it was because of the beautiful songs the little sparrows sang that did the trick!

~

The Tin Man Ghost

Did I ever tell you about the tale of the tin man ghost who carries a pail?
He carries a pail of rusty things like fenders, pans, and gypsy rings.
If you've ever heard a clanging sound, you may be sure that he's around.
He's never harmed a man or child, but lingers in crab trees or wild
dark thickets where red sumac sprouts. You may be sure he'll chase you out!
He clangs his pans and bangs his pail, and hollers with an awful wail!
They say that's why the skunk's trimmed white--he heard the tin man ghost
one night
and ran at such a frenzied pace, a line was streaked from tail to face!
The tin man ghost has left his mark upon the birch tree with white bark
when it was frightened while quite young, and now it also is among
the victims that the tin man scared, and who could trap him?
None have dared!
For he can come and go at will and bang his pans when you are still.
Some say he is a long lost-knight from some medieval battle's flight,
in panic crossed the deep wide sea and that is how he came to be
lost in the woods where you may be!
I've heard he means to do no harm, so if you hear him near a farm
or in a woods or by a bay, don't let his noise drive YOU away!

~

The Judicial Mouse

Edward was no ordinary mouse. He was a judicial mouse, for he lived in the judge's chambers in the big city hall. The judge's chambers was a most interesting place, for it boasted a wide oblong table which sometimes held morsels of doughnuts. Sometimes there was a half-eaten apple just waiting for a hungry judicial mouse to carry off and enjoy.

There were shelves and shelves of very important-looking books. At night Edward peered through the books and studied all about law, trials and the procedures of court. He thought that a judicial mouse should certainly know about law, especially since there were some mice who just did not know right from wrong.

First, there was Elmer, who was always getting into trouble. It was because of his mischievous deeds that Mr. Cook bought a mangy fierce-looking cat that roamed around the kitchen, This posed serious trouble for all the mice that lived in the city hall. If Elmer had kept his scavenging for food to night-time hours, Mr. Cook would never have seen him. But no, Elmer had to take chances and was seen scampering across the sink on more than one occasion.

Then there was Clarabelle. Someone simply must do something, the mice agreed, to put her in her place before she gave some old lady a heart attack. Clarabelle, you see, loved jumping in shopping bags that ladies carried as they came into the court chambers. She would wait until the ladies sat down, and then she would jump out!

Yes, there was need for a judicial mouse, and Edward felt that he would make a good one. It wasn't easy, studying law while living in the judge's chambers. The judge sometimes worked late at night, and Edward had to wait until he left before he could do his studying. If there were no crumbs or pieces of apple around, Edward felt it very tempting to take a bite or two out of the Wills and Orders legal papers that were scattered on the secretary's desk. Sometimes he even got so hungry that he took a bite out of the judge's law books.

During the day, Edward hid behind the heavy drapes in the judge's chambers. That way he could hear everything that went on. Finally, Edward decided he knew enough to be a bonafide judicial mouse.

The next day, Edward visited Sage Mouse, who lived in the old cupboard down the hall. Sage Mouse tested him with many questions and finally had a paper drawn up that read:

I, Mouse Sage, proclaim that Edward Mouse is hereby duly proclaimed to be an official Mouse Judge, with complete powers and authority as deemed by this high office.

Signed: Mouse Sage on This Day and This Year.

Mouse Sage placed a shiny gold seal on the paper, signed it and presented it to Edward. Millie Mouse volunteered to sew a black robe for Edward. Edward set up court right in the circuit court chambers of city hall in back of the platform where the different judges conducted their business. Edward, of course, had to wait until the chambers were empty before he could hold court.

During his court sessions, he fined Elmer mouse and made him pay three slices of cheese to the court. Elmer also had to do community service by warning anyone if and when the big fierce cat was around.

Clarabelle mouse was fined, also, and was told to stay out of ladies' shopping bags or she would be banished to the basement!

Yes, Edward was a good judicial mouse. Because of him, all the mice felt safer and were much happier. Edward solved many mouse problems which, after all, is what a good judicial mouse is supposed to do!

~

Tit For Tat

Mother calls and says to me, “You shouldn’t watch too much TV.”
Yet, she should come to school someday, for
then she’d find out right away
of all the movies we watch there, and dull TV shows we MUST bear!
~

The Man in the Moon

Little Billy loved to look up in the sky through his bedroom window to see the yellow moon beaming down very happily. He noticed that the moon seemed to have two eyes, a nose and a mouth.

"Mom," Billy asked one day, "is there really a man in the moon?"

"We like to say there is," said his mom, "because it does look that way, but it's really all pretend."

Billy listened to his mom, but he thought to himself, how does she know? I'm going to watch real close and see for myself. That night, the moon was especially full and bright, and it shone right down on Billy's bed. His room was as bright as day. Billy looked at the moon very thoughtfully. "You sure do look like a man to me," he said. He was just talking to himself, but all of a sudden his room got lighter and brighter, and a voice said, "What do you mean that I look like a man? Of course I do, for I am a man! I resent people saying that I'm not."

Billy jumped right out of bed. "Who said that?" he asked.

"Why," said the voice, "I did. I'm the Man in the Moon." The room got lighter and even brighter.

"But how can you be a man without a body?" asked Billy. "Where is the rest of you?"

"Young man," said the Man in the Moon, "the head is the most important part of the body. I don't need any other part. If I had legs, what would I do with them? With my head, I can go all around the Earth. How could I do that if I had legs and/or arms? They would be a terrible nuisance."

"I see," said Billy, but he really didn't understand. "Doesn't it get awfully boring just being in the sky all day and not being able to do anything?"

"Oh no," said the Man in the Moon, "I'm busy all the time. I am the guardian of the Earth. That means that it's my duty to watch over little girls and boys, like you."

"But why don't you shine so bright every night?" asked Billy.

"Well, if I shone every night in your area, then I couldn't watch over little girls and boys in other countries. I really have a lot to do, you see. I must be on my way now, Billy, as I have to visit the little children in China tonight, so I think it's time for you to go to bed."

Billy was feeling very sleepy and didn't have any trouble to sleep. But the next morning when he awoke, he remembered his visit from the Man in the Moon, and thought, maybe it was just all a dream. He ate his oatmeal and went out to play. He found his best friend, Donnie, and they had a lot of fun playing pirate in a clump of bushes beside the house. At dinner time Donnie went right home, but Billy didn't.

Billy was watching a bright red bird and decided to follow it to see where its nest was. He followed it as it flew from tree to tree. Down through a little meadow, he went running, following the bright red bird, and didn't even notice that it was starting to get dark. The little bird flew out of his sight, and when he turned to go back home, he suddenly realized that it was so dark that he couldn't see which way to go.

By now he was starting to get hungry as well as scared. He remembered that he hadn't even told his mom that he was going for a walk. As he was getting more and more worried, he noticed that things were getting brighter and brighter. The big full moon was rising up and over the trees.

"Oh, if you are really the Man in the Moon," begged Billy, "can you help me? I'm lost!"

"Do you believe in me?" asked the Man in the Moon, "you have to believe in order for me to help you."

"Yes, yes," said Billy, "I believe." The moon shone down on Billy and threw a bright light down upon everything. Billy began to recognize familiar places. He realized he was not as far away from home as he had thought. He looked around carefully and started running. The light from the Man in the Moon, lit the way for him to see. Just as he got to the edge of his own yard, there were his mom and dad with flashlights. They were getting ready to head to the woods to search for him.

Billy was so happy to see them that he didn't mind getting scolded for running off without telling them.

That night Man in the Moon shone through his bedroom window again. "It's a good thing," said Man in the Moon, "that I wasn't shining in China tonight, instead of here, or you might still be lost."

~

The Man in the Moon Poem

The man in the moon shines so bright in the night
That I'm happy to see such a glorious sight!
The man in the moon makes my room light as day,
And I've nothing to fear when he's smiling my way!

~

The Astronaut Mouse

It wasn't in the newspapers, but it was so. At least that is what great great great grandpa mouse told little Herman about his Uncle Kenny during the days that Cape Kennedy was a big astronaut center. This is the story told to Herman:

Everyone in Cape Kennedy knew about it. At least, every mouse in Cape Kennedy knew all about Kenny, the mouse that went to the moon and came back.

It all began when Kenny overheard flight engineers discussing a trip to the moon, after which he immediately alerted the mouse workers at the Cape. Together, they arrived at a plan and chose Kenny to be the astronaut mouse. This was not a surprising appointment as one of Kenny's ancestors had come to America with Columbus on the Santa Maria in 1492. Also, it was another relative, Cirus Mouse, who was with the expedition that found the mouth of the Mississippi River. Another relative, sHobert Mouse, had accompanied the explorer Burke into the continent of Australia long, long ago.

Kenny had to go through a rigorous training routine, from balancing exercises to weightless exercises until finally he was ready to go. Maude and Myrtle Mouse prepared mouse food for him by pressing cheese and crackers into small enough pieces for him to tuck into his space suit. He watched patiently as astronauts began entering the space capsule, and scooted in to hide among the flight bags just before the capsule door was closed.

He managed to buckle himself up to a seat where other astronauts were seated, and prepared for blast off. How exhilarating and marvelous it was! The other astronauts were so busy with their duties and controls, they never noticed Kenny. When they landed on the moon, Kenny almost met his doom. He was so anxious to put his feet on the moon that he was nearly trampled by Neil Armstrong!

In fact, Kenny's tail had been badly mangled in the near disaster, but his investigation and research was complete. He was able to return to Earth in the capsule without incident, and was hailed as a hero, for he had proved without a doubt that the moon definitely was not made out of Green Cheese!

~

From Another View

A fuzzy worm, crossing a quiet road,
The gruesome sight of one unlucky toad.
A tiny stone imbedded in cement
A teensy flower with its petals bent.
A gopher's home, and "alligator" tracks
Small pits in asphalt, every crook and crack.
These things and more, some people never see
Unless you are a little tyke, just three!

~

Wilbur and the Chicken Coop

It was a very neat chicken coop, because Farmer Briggs liked to keep everything around his farm neat and clean. Wilbur Mouse lived happily in a corner underneath the chickens' roost. There, in a corner where straw was stacked, Wilbur made himself a comfortable nest.

The chickens knew Wilbur lived in the coop with them, and didn't seem to mind. They liked his company because every night he would sing a lullaby, and the chickens would close their eyes, bury their heads under their wings and go to sleep.

However, Freddy the rooster was jealous of Wilbur. He didn't think a mouse belonged in his chicken coop, and told Wilbur that several times a day.

One evening when Wilbur was in the middle of singing a lullaby, Freddy pounced on him. The hens squawked in fright and soon Farmer Briggs came out to the coop with his flashlight and a pitchfork to see what was going on. When he poked around the coop with his pitchfork, he noticed Freddy's nest and started poking it. Wilbur managed to scoot out the door just in time, barely missing being stabbed by the pitchfork.

Shivering with fright, Wilbur buried himself in the thick branches of a lilac bush, not knowing what to do. The next day, Wilbur watched as Freddy strutted cockily around the chicken yard. He shivered as rain poured down on him and he longed for the cozy bed of straw in the coop. That night he pulled some dry leaves over himself to keep warm. He missed hearing the pitter patter of rain on the tin roof of the chicken coop.

Even through the rain Wilbur could hear the hens in the coop. They were cackling and cackling and not going to sleep like they usually did. Farmer Briggs came out several times that night, and the next, to try to find out what was going on.

One night after several days had gone by, and Wilbur had nestled down to go to sleep, he realized that someone was calling his name.

"Wilbur! Wilbur," the voice called. Carefully Wilbur crept out of his little nest, making sure that Farmer Briggs was not around.

"Oh Wilbur," said Freddy the rooster who was outside of the coop and standing not far from him. "I am so sorry for being mean to you," he said. "I know that Farmer Briggs will clip my wings if he sees me out here, but I just have to beg you to please come back to the coop. The hens have been grouchy and cranky ever since you left. They won't go to sleep, and I think it's because they miss your singing." Farmer Briggs seems to think it is ME keeping everyone awake and noisy! For all I know, he might be planning to make rooster soup out of me!"

"Well," said Wilbur, "you gave me an awful scare, you know."

"Wilbur," begged Freddy Rooster, "I promise from now on that if you move back inside the coop, I will never bother you again. I just want you to come back and start singing your lullabies again."

Wilbur was happy to move back into the coop. If ever you are on a farm, and go near the chicken coop in the evening, listen carefully for you just might hear Wilbur singing the chickens to sleep with his beautiful lullabies!

~

Christmas In the Woods

While strolling through the woods one night, I heard small creatures say,
"We must prepare ourselves, for soon will be glad Christmas Day.
Let's rid the woods of clutter, pick up limbs and twigs and leaves
And make the woods a pleasant place beneath the forest trees."
"What can I do?" the blue jay asked, "is there a task for me?"
"Oh yes, fair bird, you can announce our plans to all you see."
"And how," asked chipmunk, "can I help? I'd like to do a chore."
"Well you, dear chipmunk, can supply some acorns from your store."
And so the creatures far and wide began to gather food
And as they worked together, they were in a festive mood
Until, at last, was Christmas night and all sat down to pray
And then they gathered for a feast to share on Christmas Day.

~

The Tomato Man

"I won't drink that awful stuff! I won't! I won't! I won't!" Sally shook her curls angrily as she pushed aside a big glass of tomato juice that her mother had poured for breakfast.

"I hate juice! I hate it!" and she made such an awful fuss that her mother sighed and put the juice away. Sally smiled and started to eat her breakfast like a good girl. As she was eating her oatmeal, she noticed that the glass of juice seemed to be bubbling. Something, it seemed, was fizzing out of the glass! Suddenly a little red man jumped out of the glass and landed on the countertop.

"Who are you?" asked Sally, very startled.

"I'm the Tomato Man," said the little red man, and he turned cartwheels all over the top of the sink. "I'm glad you didn't drink me, for now I am going to go on a trip to the countryside!" With that, Tomato Man leaped off the countertop and skipped out the door.

"Wait! Wait!" Sally called, "can I go with you?" She had never seen such a little man before, and was so surprised and curious that she wanted to follow him.

"Come along if you want to," said Tomato Man as he started to skip along the path. Sally had a hard time keeping up with him. Together they ran down the path, through the garden, around the lawn, and finally down a sandy path that led through a leafy forest.

"Oh," cried Sally, "I'm getting tired. Can't we stop for awhile?" she asked.

"You should have drunk your juice. Look at me! I'm full of energy" said Tomato Man as he did cartwheel after cartwheel. Sally just sat and watched him, for she was quite worn out. In fact, she was getting hungry, too, and started to cry.

"Hush! Hush!" said Tomato Man, "you didn't eat your mush!" Tomato Man started running and running. Sally didn't want to be left all by herself, so she got up and started running after him.

Suddenly they were through the forest and into a clearing that held the most beautiful garden Sally had ever seen! Why, everything was lush and green with big beautiful blossoms and fruit. Sally rubbed her eyes. Everything seemed so bright! Although she was hungry, she turned her nose up at the little red shiny tomato that a tiny yellow pixie held up for her. Just as well, for the little tomato suddenly turned into a tomato man and started running away from the garden. Sally walked past a row of large green peas. Two brown pixies were standing guard and held out a long pea pod. "No thank you," said Sally, turning her nose up. Again she jumped back in alarm, for the pea pods suddenly sprang legs and started turning cartwheels down a garden row.

In the middle of the garden, tall stalks of corn were swaying and singing songs. Long green beans were waltzing on a high white fence. Among everything going on, Sally found herself flat on the ground when she tripped over a big head of cauliflower that sprang legs, shook itself angrily, and said, “Can’t you watch where you are going!”

“I’m sorry,” said Sally just as she noticed some big plump blueberries on a nearby bush. As she reached over to grab some, a purple pixie slapped her hand. “If you can’t eat peas or tomatoes, you certainly are not allowed to eat blueberries,” said an angry pea as he started running down the path. By now Sally was really, really hungry and started crying again.

“Well,” said Tomato Man, who was standing there watching everything, “If you had drunk your juice and hadn’t snubbed your nose at eating tomatoes and peas, you would have had energy like me, and you could turn cartwheels like me, too.”

“This is a silly silly place,” cried Sally. “I just want to go home!”

“Try some of this tomato juice,” said Tomato Man holding out a glass of juice for her, “and I will help you find your way home.”

In desperation, Sally held her nose and drank down the juice. “Oh, I guess it isn’t that bad,” she admitted, as she gulped down the rest. Because she was so hungry, she grabbed a little red tomato and crunched it down. “Oh,” she said, “This isn’t so bad, after all.” Next she munched on a little orange carrot. By now she was feeling energetic and happy.

The Lettuce Man was dancing up and down the garden rows, turning cartwheels all the way. At the end of a row, he joined hands with the Tomato Man and they did a jig. Sally was laughing hard until she suddenly felt something bump her arm. She looked up to see her mother bending over her.

“Sally, you fell asleep at the breakfast table,” said her mother. “If you don’t hurry, you will be late for school.”

Sally had been dreaming! But do you know that she drinks her juice every morning now, and you should see her do cartwheels!

~

Sand Castles

Water lapping at my toes
Sea spray stinging at my nose,
Can't they know I'm hard at play
Building sand castles today?

There! It's done! The final tap!
Some brave knight might need a map
To find his way in every room
And not fall in the castle's ruin.

Water lapping at my toes,
Sea spray stinging at my nose,
I see you, too, must like to play
Washing sand castles away!

~

The Time to Marry

In the woodland when it's spring
And all returning songbirds sing,
The wood mouse climbs from underground.
He yawns and stretches, looks around
Then dusts his yard of all debris
And sweeps the leaves beneath the tree
And then goes for a springtime walk
And suns himself upon a rock.
When Nature sends its first spring shower
That stirs awake each sleepy flower
Mouse knows the time is right to seek
A girlfriend mouse with rosy cheek.
He'll marry her and take her home
And seldom will they want to roam,
For everywhere when it is spring
That is the time for Marrying!

~

A Boy's Point of View

Why are girls always so sissy, always playing school or house
Always screaming off to mother if they see a little mouse?
Cannot take a little teasing, yet like to torment US, so,
Maybe girls were only made so they could give us small boys woe!

~

A Girl's Point of View

Why are boys always such nuisance, always seeming to act rough,
Always pushing, shoving, yelling, always trying to act tough?
Always catching snakes or spiders, or off building some dumb fort,
To us girls their actions make them quite a weird and motley sort!

~

A Christmas Gift From Shawn

Shawn knew that he was different. He felt it all along
He saw in people's faces that *his* features were "all wrong.
He knew it on his birthday when nobody came to play
Nobody came to play games or to share his special day.
He heard it at the doctor's, who had tapped upon his bones
and whispered, though he heard it, "I'm sorry, Mrs. Jones."
And then came Christmas season with its giving and its gifts
and everyone was giving either special hints or list.
Shawn couldn't find a present that he could give his mom,
and all that he attempted broke in his nervous palm.
Too soon was Christmas morning, but still no gift from Shawn
but just as he was waking, a thought struck him that dawn:
he had no fine wrapped package yet one thing he still could do
"Oh, Mamma, Merry Christmas! My gift is I LOVE YOU!"

~

Nasty Rasty

Nasty Rasty came today. I tried to make him go away.
He wouldn't listen, but instead, crawled right beside me in my bed!
He made me grouchy, made me frown, and turned my whole day upside down!
He made me kick my dog and cat, and on my friend he made me RAT!
I tried to run! I tried to hide! But Nasty Rasty went inside
When I went in or out again. He even lost my good ink pen!
He ripped my jeans, muddied my shoes! Cut paper dolls from father's news!
He spilled my milk, wrote on the wall, and made me cranky in the Mall!
Nasty Rasty came today. I tried to push him far away.
I hid behind the closet door, but he still found me, and what's more...
He made me scribble on the floor!
He scattered pillows, wrecked my bed, and sprinkled paint upon my head!
He even followed me to school and made me break the Golden Rule.
He made me scowl and punch and pinch and made my favorite teacher flinch!
But, oh, at last I found a way, to make old Nasty go away.
He backed up, tripped into a tree when he looked up and stared at me
And then took off and ran a mile, for I had scared him with a
S M I L E!
And I never saw him again!

~

The Tulip Tree

Things in the world of people were a lot different years ago than they are today. For instance, in the springtime when tree blossoms were out in all their glory, some of them kept their blossoms for a longer time than they do today. The Tulip Tree was one of these.

When the earth was fresh and young, the Tulip Tree was one of the first trees to blossom and one of the last to lose them. But like some human beings, the Tulip Tree was boastful of its blooms. This ended up with the other trees being jealous!

"Look at me!" said the Tulip Tree as it gently waved its beautiful blossoming branches to and fro. "I'll bet you wish you had blossoms like me," she would say as little golden daffodils growing around the tree waved their yellow petals.

"I'll bet you wish you could keep your blossoms as long as I do," crooned the Tulip Tree. Daffodils and narcissus waved their little petals and tried to ignore the Tulip tree, for they knew their time of blossoming was short, indeed. They resented the Tulip Tree bragging so much.

They did not like the way she boasted, either, and complained to Mother Carey.

"Mother Carey," they pleaded, "something needs to be done about the Tulip Tree. She is so boastful of her long-lasting beautiful petals that she makes the rest of us feel awful."

Mother Carey had been so busy organizing the spring festivals all over the world that she had not been paying attention to some things. She decided that maybe she had better visit the Tulip Tree to see what was going on.

Sure enough, there was Tulip Tree waving her branches and boasting about how long she kept her blossoms. Mother Carey had allowed the Tulip Tree to keep her blossoms for so long as she thought it would help to keep people cheerful, especially after a long cold winter. However, she was not pleased with Tulip Tree's boastful manner. "Hmm," she said to herself. "I will have to come up with a solution."

Sometimes when one is trying to come up with a good solution for a problem, it is a good thing to discuss the matter with others. Thus it was that Mother Carey called a meeting of the Spring Festival Committee.

The North Wind attended the meeting even though she was getting ready to go south. The Warm Zephyr came although he was impatient to get on with his duties of melting the snow that still remained after the cold winter. Mother Sun beamed down and made her presence known, although she, too, was anxious to continue her task of warming the soil and flower beds. Uncle Rain came although he was a little late. He had been busy supervising the rains that were now beginning to fall in the northeast.

Aunt Snow attended although she was very tired from the long winter and was anxious to take a nap. Brother Frost came, too, even though he had been busy filling buckets with frost.

"The Tulip Tree," began Mother Carey, "is very boastful and is hurting the feelings of others." As the committee gathered around her, she continued, "We need to find a way to gently discourage her from displaying so much vanity."

"I could drown her with rain," suggested Uncle Rain. He was anxious to get back to the northeast and was impatient to end the meeting.

"I could blow down her branches," suggested the North Wind who was also a little irritated in this interruption of his schedule.

"I could wilt her blossoms," said Mother Sun, although she herself did not like the idea.

"Brother Frost," Mother Carey asked, "you didn't suggest anything. Do you have any ideas?"

Brother Frost was still a little sleepy from his long winter sleep and hadn't listened to the other suggestions. He jumped with a start when he heard Mother Carey talking to him.

"Well," he said, scratching his head in thought, "the Tulip Tree is beautiful. Maybe we could somehow just shorten her time of blossoming. I could send in a crew to brown her blossoms after a few days of blooming. That way she could continue to show her blossoms but for a shorter time."

"Hmm," said the committee in one voice. "That might not be a bad idea."

Mother Carey nodded her head in agreement. "Yes," she said, that might be a solution, as we don't want to permanently damage Tulip Tree. The world of people love her very much. We just want to shorten her blossoming time so she will stop bragging so much."

So it was that from that day forward, every Tulip Tree in Mother Carey's kingdom shows her beautiful blossoms for a very short time before they start to turn brown and fall to the ground. As you drive down any street where a Tulip Tree is in blossom, you will notice that one day it is beautiful and the next day all the blossoms are gone!

~

A Different Song for Jimmy

Jimmy had just turned ten when he heard his grandma say, "I worry about that boy.
He doesn't seem to play
or do the things that all kids, do, nor get along
with anyone. He seems to sing a different song.
What will become of him?" And then she closed the door. Try as he may,
he couldn't hear her any more.
Did they mean him? Was he that different, after all? He pulled his jacket off
and curled up in the hall.
That was his favorite place to keep his stuff, or sleep. He felt secure with
all his blankets in a heap
upon the floor. And was it wrong to be alone? He liked a darkened room,
away from lights that shone.
So what, he thought, if other kids liked other things for which he didn't care
about. If he had wings
he'd soar above whoever didn't understand and then fly high until he found
a secret land!
He knew his mother worried; and he had no dad. He went to special schooling
which really wasn't bad.
His mom thought him too thin. He picked at things to eat and rocked when
they went driving, or in whatever seat,
and couldn't stop the rocking, no matter how he tried. He saw his mother
watching. And sometimes she cried.
He had a favorite grandpa who took him here and there. Sometimes they
would play chess. He tried hard to play fair.
As years went on, he grew up tall and smarter than his years. He still liked
darkened rooms, and still had many fears.
He learned to play the flute. He played it very well. And everyone who
heard, were very quick to tell
that everyone has talents, no matter how it seems, and everyone can use them
to seek their special dreams.

~

It Pays to Listen

"You may go out," said Mother Snake, "but watch for Billy Brown.
He's sure to come around today. Keep watchful for his sound!"
"So who's afraid?" thought Junior sliding through a violet bed.
He never HEARD the pillowcase that slipped upon his head!

At lunchtime Billy left the case upon a backyard chair
And little snake fell out and felt the freedom of warm air.
He wiggled back to swampland, to the safety of his nest,
And practiced on his listening, then curled up for a rest.

And sure enough, when Billy Brown came through the swamps next day
The little snake COULD hear his steps, and slithered far away!

~

Teamwork for Tommy

Tommy Mouse loved the wide green field. There was so much to do and so much to see. He had a lot of friends that he played with who lived in the fields.

One day while Tommy was playing the field a dark shadow swooped overhead. "What was that?" asked Tommy to no one in particular.

Before he had time to think, the dark shadow swooped down again, so close that he could feel the flutter of wings.

"Buzzard!" shouted Jimmy, one of Tommy's friends, just as the big buzzard swooped down and nabbed Jimmy by his tail.

"Help!" yelled Jimmy, but fortunately for him, when the buzzard leaned sideways to miss hitting a tree, he dropped little Jimmy into the grass.

"Run for your life," yelled Jimmy as he fell to the ground, quickly rolled over and slid down into a hole with Tommy right behind him.

"Who's in my house?" asked a gruff voice as Jimmy and Tommy tumbled into the dark hole.

"It's us! Jimmy and Tommy!" said the little mice together.

"Well, you shouldn't go tumbling into someone's house without knocking. Have you no manners?" asked the gruff voice again.

Now that Tommy's eyes were getting used to the darkness, he saw that the voice came from a fat brown mole who was busy sweeping up the dirt that had tumbled into the hole along with them.

"Since you're here, and even though you weren't invited," said the mole, "my name is Willie. I suppose you might like something to eat?"

"Yes, yes," said Tommy and Jimmy. They were always hungry and never turned away an invitation for food. While eating their grubs and insects, the mice told Willie what had happened.

"My, my," mused Willie. "It sounds to me like you both nearly met your doom before you found my room! Hey, that rhymes! Got it? Doom and room?" Willie rolled over in laughter.

Tommy and Jimmy didn't laugh. They didn't see anything funny about nearly being eaten by a buzzard!

"I tell you what," said Willie, once he recovered his dignity, "I'll let you slide down any of my holes any time you want to, as long as you promise to be on the lookout for ME when I'm gathering food for the winter. Is that a deal?"

"That sounds good to me," said Tommy, and from that day on, whenever big buzzards or hawks came swooping over, Tommy and Jimmy both watched out for buzzards and hawks, and warned Willie if they saw one coming.

"This is team work," said Tommy happily as the three of them feasted on walnut shells stuffed full of all kinds of good food. As far as I know, they haven't been caught yet by a buzzard or a hawk!

~

Fridays are Crappy

"On Fridays, kids often get mean!
They kick and swear and bully,"
said Logan to his aunt one day.
"And girls act so unruly!
The teacher doesn't seem to care.
I hate to go to school!"
said Logan, talking on and on,
saying that kids were cruel!
"Let's think," his aunt said, "what to do
to keep you safe and happy."
"It's hopeless!" Logan shook his head.
"Fridays are just plain crappy!"
"Don't let those kids know how you feel,"
his aunt went on to say,
"pretend they just don't bother you,
in time they'll stay away."
And as it was, as time went by,
the bullies that were bad
began to leave Logan alone
which made Logan quite glad!
Now, Fridays seemed like much more fun,
for as his aunt would say,
"if you are patient long enough,
problems will go away!"

~

Sometimes Wishes Do Come True

Once upon a time there were three rabbits who lived happily together in a rose- covered cottage. There was baby bunny, mother rabbit, and father rabbit. Together they went for walks through the fields of daisies, gardens and leafy woods.

They played games together and had good times. But then one day something happened.

Mother and father rabbit started fighting and arguing all the time. They went to see a judge and decided to get a divorce. They both wanted baby bunny Lenny, to live with them although they both would be living in separate places.

The judge listened to them both and made a decision. "I decree," he said, that Lenny should live with his father."

Mother rabbit cried. Lenny cried. But there was nothing they could do. Mother rabbit handed baby Lenny over to his father.

Lenny did not understand. He missed his mother and cried long tears far into the night. His mother would come and take him for a visit once in awhile, but it was never enough for Lenny. He did not like living with his father.

After awhile, Lenny's father brought home a new wife. Soon there were several cribs full of other little babies. Lenny felt left out. He was not happy at all. He did not like his stepmother. He missed his own mother. When no one was looking, he pinched his little brothers and sisters. They would cry and he would get scolded.

He refused to eat his dinner. He put muddy prints on the walls. He kicked everybody, including a little dog that sometimes came to visit, and he even called his stepMother names! Of course he got many scoldings and "time outs."

When he got to see his mother, he complained and cried. Of course this made his mother very sad. But there was nothing anyone could do.

One day Lenny had a dream that he was in a big castle. It was full of beautiful things. Suddenly he saw King Rabbit who said: "Lenny, why are you making everyone unhappy?"

Lenny told him that he missed his mother and did not like living with his dad.

"Son," said King Rabbit, "there are many things in the world that are wanted but cannot be had. Look at the swan who might lose his mate and has to live by himself the rest of his life. He doesn't cry about it. Look at the owl who loses his home when the field crows swoop down to destroy it. Even the great elephant has to live in a smaller jungle because a lot of it has been cut down. He doesn't cry about it.

"You need to be patient and things will work out after awhile," said King Rabbit. "Maybe the day will come when you can live with your mother again. Until then try to be happy and patient." And then King Rabbit whispered something in Lenny's ear.

When he woke up, Lenny remembered the dream. From then on he quit calling his stepmother names. He quit crying and complaining and quit pinching his brothers and sisters. He tried hard to be patient. He was still unhappy but he tried hard not to show it.

One day, several years later, Lenny met his mother for their usual visit and she said, "Lenny, you are allowed to come and live with me now." Lenny was very happy. He smiled as he remembered the dream he had had years ago, and of the words whispered in his ear by King Rabbit.

King Rabbit had whispered: "Never give up on your dreams, but while you are waiting, be patient, be kind, smile, and DON'T KICK THE DOG!"

~

The Little Old Woman Who Liked Pots and Pans

There was an old woman who lived down the lane. She lived all alone, and she ate her toast plain.

She lived all alone, that is but for her cat who pestered her so much, she named it "Now Scat!"

Now Scat and the woman had little to do. She played the piano or made Irish stew.

She washed clothes and hung them outside on the line, or sat in her rocking chair under the pine.

Her husband was gone, and her children were grown. They lived far away each with homes of their own.

She sent letters off to them, sometimes a small gift. She loved to go shopping. It gave her a "lift."

She went to garage sales, flea markets and such. She had little money, could not afford much.

She purchased old pans, some were of stainless steel, in which she fed Now Scat his favorite meal.

She liked to go shopping for "just one more pan." "Now here is a good one," she said to the man,

The man who took pennies for pots, pans and such. For each of these items, she didn't pay much.

Some pots were for chicken, some pots were for stew. Some black pots and blue pots, none of them new.

One day the old woman pulled open a drawer when pots, pans, and dishes fell out with a ROAR!

The blue pots! The black pots! Old gray pans, and green! Now Scat ran in fright from this terrible scene!

Just then at the door came a man and small boys. "Please ma'm. We're in need of some goods or some toys."

They looked at the pots and pans scattered about. The floor was quite covered! No spot appeared bare!

"It seems I have too many pans and, yes, pots!" "I see," said the stranger, "looks like you have lots!"

"I could spare a few, she said, starting to stack the pots and the pans and the lids on a rack.

She gathered a bunch and then said to the man, "Here, take some," and handed him each color of pan.

The man and the boys were quite pleased with their gear, said "Thank you," and left. Soon the woman could hear

The laughter of children as lids became drums. The street became noisy with Rum Ta Ta Tums!

The old woman turned, settled back in her chair. Now Scat curled beside
her with hardly a care
And both were content with the Very Good Deed of sharing their treasures
with people in need!

~

Kaylee, the "Wanna Be" Princess

Kaylee read about a princess and wondered, "could it be
that something so exciting, could it happen to me?
If I could be a princess," and she began to dream
of what her life would be like, and what it all could mean.
"I'd have the best of dresses, and wear a silver crown,
and, oh, how I would glitter with sequins on my gown!
I'd go to all the dances, eat cookies, chocolate cake,
and dance with maids-in-waiting, go sailing on the lake."
Well, Kaylee went on dreaming and said to all she knew,
"When I become a princess, oh, all the things I'll do."
Her friends soon grew quite tired of hearing Kaylee talk
of when she'd be a princess, and they began to balk.
"We can't stand her!" they chattered, and ran when she would call.
"Well! I will not invite THEM to any dance or ball!"
With that, she snatched some cookies mom baked just for Kaylee
and took her book and blanket and curled up by a tree.
Again she started dreaming of lands far far away
where she, a little princess, was dressed in grand array.
Her gown sparkled with bangles and shiny threads of gold
and tables lined the hallway with pastries creamed and rolled.
"This must be truly heaven," thought Kaylee as she twirled
while brightly costumed dancers about her turned and swirled.
She "oohed" and "ah'd" in wonder. "This must be some estate!
Oh, I think being a princess, is something really great!"
She stuffed herself with cream rolls and danced from night to day.
Her friends would be so jealous! She'd tell them right away!
She searched for casual clothing so she could play outside.
"Oh, no," a maid said to her. "A princess must abide
by rules of dress and manners. It would not do at all
if you would run and play hard and maybe have a fall!
Now it is time for lessons. There's much for you to do.
You might have time for fun things, when all your chores are through."
And so she studied lessons until the day was done
and soon became impatient to play outside and run.
"Oh no," her maid-in-waiting said as she reached the door.
"A princess needs a chaperone and anyway, what's more,
a princess cannot wander alone or to the store."
Soon Kaylee got to thinking, "this life is sure be a bore!"
"Then can my friends come visit?" she asked the maid again."
"Oh, no! Oh, dear! They cannot!" And while she spoke, just then

the footman brought some goodies, and Kaylee grabbed a bunch!
It made her feel less lonesome as she began to munch
and munch until her head hurt. Her stomach hurt some, too.
Her gown felt hot and stuffy. Her shoes hurt, being new.
"This is NO fun!" she blurted out. "I wish I was just ME!"
And in a FLASH, it happened! She was, again, Kaylee!
She looked about quite startled, then ran to find a friend!
"I'm glad I'm NOT a princess! I'm glad I'm me!" The End!

~

The Granite Family

Long before Sasquatch inhabited the forest, creatures of a far different kind lived on the earth. They were strong and fearless and lived mostly in the western part of the United States. The climate, long ago, was different than it is today, and many strange and wild animals roamed the earth. But these creatures could deal with them because, you see, they were made of granite.

There was one family that was especially interesting. That was the family of Kcor who was vey powerful and mighty. He moved slowly, being so heavy, but his power enabled him to pull up big trees by their roots. This was no easy task because trees and ferns were immense in size and made trees of today look like ant trees.

Then there was Redluod who was daintier. She could move heavy things around but needed Kcor to help her. Enots tried to imitate both Kcor and Redluod and did pretty good for his age and size.

Kcor, Redluod and little Enots loved the country under the huge rainforest ferns. They liked to watch the dinosaurs that made such interesting noises. When dinosaurs fought with each other, Redluod and Enots both got quite scared. It seemed so cruel because who ever won the dinosaur battle would eat the loser! Enots couldn't understand why it had to be that way.

Enots loved the land they lived on. The sky was heavy with mist and steam. Huge flowers draped over everything. Enots and his parents would stand under them and admire the big colorful blooms. They also loved the big lakes and enjoyed the coolness of the water.

Enots' family, however, knew that these good times would not last. They could sense that the earth was changing. The climate seemed to get different every day. Kcor

taught Enots to enjoy each day, telling him that happiness could only be measured in minutes, not years. Nothing, Kcor said, lasts forever. It's important to be happy where you are, and not to wish for something else.

Sure enough, the Day of Separation eventually happened. Kcor knew it was happening when he saw the sun slip behind the clouds and did not come out for awhile. The whole earth seemed to stand still as great thunder erupted from the sky and heavy rain came down so fast and hard that the lakes started spilling over and covering everything. Then the earth started shivering and shaking. The great trees started tumbling to the ground. The giant ferns fell over and crashed in the tall grasses. Great animals were stopped dead in their tracks.

Kcor, Enots and Redloub were all part of the great earth family. When the earth stopped shaking, they were scattered all over the place and can still be seen today. If you drive through Oregon along Route 84, you can still see Redloub happily soaking up the sun. Along the wide Columbia River you can see the granite hand of Kcor, reaching for the sun, and you can see the foot of Enots in Olympia rain forests as he stands on his head on the Great Earth. As you might have guessed, Kcor, Enots and Redloub were rocks, stones and boulders, and if you travel along the western coast of the United States, you can see a lot of them scattered everywhere where they came to rest when the Day of Separation ended. You will be glad to know they are all happily soaking up the sun!

~

Where is the Moon?

"Mom, where is the moon? I don't see it tonight.
I looked and I looked and it's nowhere in sight.
The night seems so dark, and the sky is so black.
I miss my friend, Moon. Will it ever come back?"
"Well, son," said his mom, "Some things change, some do not!
The moon, just like you, never stays in one spot.
It depends where it is when the night starts to fall.
You see it some nights, but on some, not at all.
It gibbons when growing until it is fat,
And that's how you like it, as plump as a cat!
And then it starts waning until it is gone.
You see but its shadow when in sneaks the dawn.
But if it was full every night, what a bore!
You'd soon tire of seeing it, that I am sure."
Mike looked out the window, then sat on his bed.
"Well, since I can't see it, I'll sketch it instead!
And he did!

Can you sketch the phases of the moon?

~

Claude Seagull

Claude loved the crystal cold shimmering waters of Lake Superior. He loved the way the warm rays of the sun bounced off the crashing waves, bouncing off his back when he swam.

The sandy beaches were full of tasty morsels for a seagull, and the lake held a myriad of different fish that he could easily swoop down and catch. He was one happy seagull.

Claude's Mother told him that he was a quick learner. In fact, she told him that he was the smartest one in her big brood of family. It did seem that he could swim faster and fly higher than anyone else. He could easily out-race all of his brothers.

"Slow down," said his mother one day. "You'll never have any friends if you keep trying to be better than everyone else."

"Ah Mom," said Claude, "I can't help it if I'm fast," and he kept up with his old ways. But he noticed that everyone did seem to avoid him and after awhile, he started feeling lonely.

"I just won't let them know how I feel," he told himself. As time went on, he decided it just wasn't fun looking for fish all by himself. He had found a new hobby.

He noticed that when People came, they would often drop some of their food. He found People food to be quite tasty.

"No, Claude," his mother said, "People food will get you into trouble. You must stay away from it."

"Don't worry about me, Mom," said Claude as he secretly flew over to where some People were having a picnic. He fluffed his wings and watched as People scattered, leaving many crumbs behind.

Soon, Claude became very popular. People started taking pictures of him. "I'm famous," he told himself as he preened around the sandy beach in front of a People family.

"It's time to come with us, Claude," said his mother one cool day. "We are flying south and you need to come, too."

"No, Mom," said Claude. "I can fly fast and catch up with you. So you go ahead and don't worry about me." He had his eye on a family of People that had a big picnic basket.

Sure enough there were a lot of tasty potato chips and crackers that he could munch on. This was so much easier than catching fish, he thought. As he looked up he saw his mom and all the other seagulls soar high up into the sky until finally they were out of sight. "I'll catch up with them later," Claude told himself.

But as days went on, he found he had gained so much weight from eating so much People food, that it was hard to fly. The air was getting colder and colder. Fewer People came to the beach. Claude poked around campgrounds and garbage dumps, trying to find a few scraps.

"Wow," he said to himself, "what a gold mine," as he poked through garbage bags at a big dump site. But as days went by and the weather got colder and colder, Claude found that he couldn't peck hard enough to get any food out of the bags because they were frozen!

The night brought a heavy storm of ice and snow. Claude curled up to sleep and tried to stay warm. The cold wind blew over everything and all became still, silent and frozen. Nothing stirred. Along the beach was a sign laying on the ground. The sign read: Please Do Not Feed the Seagulls.

~

Millie, The Traveling Cow

Millie, a brown and white cow, wanted to travel. She stood in the pasture along the freeway and watched as cars and trucks whizzed by.

"I wonder where they are going?" she asked no one in particular. The other cows in the pasture were contentedly eating grass and chewing their cud, but not Millie.

"Oh, how I would love to travel on the highway," she said to herself.

One day Farmer Joe parked his truck in the pasture while he went about getting ready to take things into town. Millie noticed that he had left the truck tailgate down as he walked away. She decided this was her chance! She looked around. No one was looking. Quietly, she moseyed over to the truck. Sure that no one saw her, she made a big jump.

Ker Wump! Millie landed in the back of the truck! She quickly hid herself behind several big bales of hay. "I'll hide back here until we get started," she said, "then I can look out the window." It was awhile before Farmer Joe came back, and Millie was getting restless. "Where is he?" she wondered, but soon there he came with an armful of bales of hay. He never noticed Millie in the back of the truck. She crouched down behind the hay. Farmer Joe slammed the tailgate shut.

In a few minutes the truck lunged and started on its way. Bumpity, bump, bump, went the truck, bouncing along the bumpy dirt road.

"Ohhh," moaned Millie. "I didn't know it would be so bumpy." She was starting to feel sick and her hoofs kept sliding on the slippery truck floor. Finally, the truck came to the highway and picked up in speed.

"So this is how it feels," thought Millie. Despite her stomach being queasy, she felt pleased and thrilled. Farmer Joe drove on and on. Millie was starting to feel more and more restless. She wanted to *see* where they were going. There was a small window in the back of the truck just behind Farmer Joe's seat. Millie started peering out the window.

"Ah," she said. "I can see the world!" But now her stomach was feeling worse. The thrill of riding in a truck was starting to lose its fun. Maybe it was time to go home!

Just then, Farmer Joe looked up at the rear view window and saw Millie facing him from the back of the truck! "What?" he exclaimed. He screeched the truck to a stop.

"Millie," he said, "how did you get back there?"

"Moo," said Millie, which meant, "can we go back home now?" She gave Farmer Joe a woeful look.

"Well, Millie," said Farmer Brown, "I don't know how you got back there but I need to go to town and you will just have to stay put until I am done there!" He didn't sound very pleased!

"Moo," said Millie again, meaning "Thank you!" Farmer Joe made sure she was comfortable, and propped up several bales of hay so she wouldn't fall.

Finally they got to town and Farmer Joe took care of all his errands. Millie was glad to see him come back to the truck so they could start for home. She didn't look out the window any more. Her stomach hurt and her feet hurt. She just wanted to be home!

When Farmer Joe pulled into the farmyard, he opened the tailgate and let her out.

From then on, Millie didn't watch the cars and trucks speed by on the highway. She was happy to be in her own pasture, eating fresh grass. She was done with traveling and decided there is no place like home!

~

Just for You!

Did you know that grapes are blue,
Green or purple colored, too
And they grow upon green vines!
Did you know that peanuts hide
In their brown shells deep inside
And they grow beneath the earth!
Did you know potatoes grow
Underground in row by row
Then a shovel digs them up!
Did you know that pumpkins are
Very first a golden star
Then they're green, and then they're orange!
And the pickles that you eat
Were cucumbers green and sweet
Packed in spices in a jar!
All these things and many more
Come from Mother Nature's magic store!

~

Millie's Second Adventure

You know how it is when you say you will never do something again, but then you do it? It was that way with Millie, the cow.

Millie had said she would be content to stay in her own pasture and not travel anymore after her last experience of riding in Farmer Joe's truck. But one day she got restless again.

"It gets so boring being in the pasture all day," she said wistfully while looking over the fence. There was a wide green field on the other side of the fence, where daisies bloomed, their little white heads nodding in the summer breeze.

"I wonder," said Millie aloud, "what it would feel like to wander across the field and go for a walk through all those lovely daisies."

"Millie," said Betsy Cow, who was standing beside her, "are you day dreaming again?" Betsy was a little younger than Millie, and thought Millie was the greatest cow in the world.

"Well," said Millie thoughtfully, "it would be so nice to be able to go walking in the daisy field."

Betsy looked over the fence. Being shorter than Millie, she couldn't see much. Also, Betsy was near sighted. "Oh, I don't know," she said, "I feel real safe being right here."

Millie didn't say anything. She just kept staring out at the next field and wondering how she could get over the fence.

The next day, in between eating and chewing her cud, Millie walked up and down the fencerow. She was looking for a place where she could get over or under it.

She walked all the way to the north end of the fencerow and all the way to the east. By the time she got to the south end, she had to lie down and rest awhile, but she didn't give up her idea of walking through the field of daisies.

Suddenly, almost to the end of the south fence pole, she noticed that a section of the fence was down, with part of it on the ground. Millie looked around. "No," she said to herself, "I better not cross over right now or Farmer Joe will see me. I'll wait until it's dark."

Millie slowly walked back to where Betsy was chewing her cud. She told her what she planned to do. "Can I go along?" asked Betsy. "Pretty please?"

Millie looked at Betsy and decided that she, too, should be allowed to have some adventure in life. "Okay," said Millie. "Let's both rest here for now and when night falls and the stars are bright, we will go exploring."

"Oh, wonderful!" exclaimed Betsy. She could hardly contain her excitement.

That evening when darkness fell, the cows gathered together under a tree. All, that is, except Millie and Betsy. They stayed in the far end of the field, but Farmer Joe was so anxious to get to a cub scout meeting for his son that evening, that he never noticed that Millie and Betsy were not with the rest of the herd.

Soon, night stars started coming out one by one. "Now's the time," said Millie as they looked up at the sky full of bright stars. She and Betsy got up and started walking slowly to the south end of the fencerow. "Here's the place," said Millie as she and Betsy stepped carefully across the downed fence.

Before they knew it, they were both strolling through the field of daisies. Millie thought it was the most wonderful feeling in the world. Soon they crossed the field and came to Farmer Smith's house next door to Farmer Joe. They walked across his yard, went up to the house and peered through the window. Farmer Smith and his wife were both asleep in bed.

"Oh," said Betsy while bending down to smell a purple Johnny Jump Up. "This is SO beautiful!" She let out a big MOO of joy!

"Quiet, Betsy!" said Millie. You'll wake Farmer Smith. But it was too late.

"I think I just heard a cow moo," said Farmer Smith, jumping out of bed in time to see Millie and Betsy standing in the middle of Farmer Smith's wife's flower garden.

"Oh, no!" he said loudly, "Farmer Joe's cows are loose." He quickly telephoned Farmer Joe the bad news.

Farmer Joe was not happy to be roused out of bed in the middle of the night, nor was he happy when he had to get dressed to go out and bring Millie and Betsy back home.

"Millie," said Farmer Joe, as he coaxed her and Betsy into the big truck so he could haul them home. "When will you ever learn?"

Millie and Betsy were both quiet as they were taken back home, but when they were back in their own field, Betsy said, "Oh Millie, that was the most wonderful adventure ever!"

~

Millie Goes Wading

It was a very hot summer day and there wasn't much shade in Farmer Joe's pasture. The cows huddled under a few trees in the middle of the pasture, but there wasn't enough room for Millie to be under there, too.

"Oh, how I wish," thought Millie, "that I could wade in a nice cool water hole. How good that would feel!"

There were no water holes in Farmer Joe's fields. Each day seemed to be hotter than the day before. It was so hot that Farmer Joe's wife didn't hang out her clothes on the line like she usually did because the heat made the clothes too hard to iron. Farmer Joe's wife hated to iron!

It was so hot that Farmer Joe's vegetable garden was starting to dry up. The corn wouldn't tassel, and the peas dried right in their green pods! Even the lawn was starting to turn brown. When Farmer Joe's wife tried to dig some onions out of the garden, the soil was so hard and dry that the tops of the onions broke off but the onions stayed in the hard ground.

It was so hot that most people stayed indoors and went outside only when they absolutely had to! It was so hot that Millie, along with the rest of the cows, started to feel sick.

Farmer Joe was watching all of this and decided that something had to be done. Then he had an idea.

The next day a big grader came into Farmer Joe's field. "Where do you want me to dig?" asked the grader operator.

"How about in that corner over there," said Farmer Joe, pointing to an area in the cow pasture. "Dig it so that it will be big enough for the cows but not too deep. I don't want any of my cows to drown."

"Cows?" Millie heard the magical word. She watched as the grader started digging. Soon water started seeping into the hole that was created. Millie walked over and watched the hole starting to fill up with the cold water.

A pond, as you know, can be a dangerous place. Millie was very careful, once the hole was dug, not to go in too deep. Farmer Joe stood at the edge of the pond watching as the cows headed to the water, one by one.

How good the water felt! Millie was afraid to go in over her knees, but, oh, how wonderful it was! sFarmer Joe watched the cows as they all went wading. He felt good seeing them look so happy. But no one was happier than Millie!

~

Millie Goes to the County Fair

"Where's everyone going?" asked Millie as she saw a group of cows heading towards the barn and Farmer Joe's big truck.

"Oh," said Bonnie Cow, "farmer Joe is taking them to the County Fair."

"Fair?" asked Millie. "What is a Fair?"

"A Fair," explained Bonnie Cow, "is where farmers from all over the area take their farm crops, animals, and vegetables to be judged and admired."

"Why would they do that?" asked Millie. "People can come right here and see us."

"It's like a competition," explained Bonnie. "I went to the Fair once. The best animals and vegetables get ribbons." Bonnie was older than Millie and knew about such things.

"Did you get a ribbon?" asked Millie.

"Yes, I did. I got a blue one," said Bonnie Cow. A blue ribbon is s the best kind of ribbon to get as it means First Place. A red ribbon means Second Place, and a white ribbon means Third Place.

"Where is this ribbon?" asked Millie. "I don't remember seeing it."

"Gerald Goat ate it before we even got home. He got one, too, but ate that one as well," said Bonnie shaking her head. "Farmer Joe was rather upset about it, but there was nothing to do about it."

"Hmm," said Millie, "I wonder how I could get to go to the Fair." The idea of a blue ribbon sounded very nice, and she was eager to get one.

"If you really want to go," said Bonnie, "then line up with the other cows and maybe Farmer Joe will let you go, too."

Millie walked over to the other cows gathered by the big truck and followed the others getting in.

"Millie," said Farmer Joe when he spotted her standing in the back of the truck. "What are you doing back there?" But it was too late to try to get Millie out as the other cows had huddled in front of her.

Millie hoped she wouldn't be sick again from riding in a truck. She tried to concentrate on winning a blue ribbon.

Soon the cows were unloaded onto the Fairgrounds and were led into a big long building with lots of other cows. A big rope was tied around Millie's neck as she was led to a stall. Although she didn't like the rope idea, she was still excited. How great it would be to get a blue ribbon!

Before long a lot of people came in and started walking up and down the aisles between the cows. Little children stopped to pet the cows, but some children poked their fingers into Millie's hide. Millie didn't like to be poked.

The judges came in and started looking at the cows and hanging ribbons here and there on the fence posts. Millie couldn't tell if she got one or not. As the week wore on, Millie was getting more and more bored. It was hot and stuffy in the building and she longed to go outside again. Sometimes her water bucket was empty and she couldn't get anything to drink.

One little boy pulled her tail so hard that it hurt! "Maybe," thought Millie to herself, "this Fair business is not so great after all."

"It's time to go home now," said Farmer Joe when he finally came by. He loaded the cows back onto the big truck. As he did so, Millie noticed that he clutched a handful of ribbons. "Gerald Goat won't eat THESE ribbons," he said as he laid the ribbons on the seat beside him in the truck.

Millie somehow knew one of those blue ribbons belonged to her, and she was happy that she had actually made it to the great County Fair!

~

Millie Finds a Friend

Millie was lonely. Oh, she had the company of the other cows, but something was missing. She didn't know what it was, but she felt lonely.

Some of her friends had baby calves. She thought the little calves looked so cute. But Millie wasn't old enough to have a calf of her own. She watched the other cows with their calves and thought how nice it must be to have someone to love.

"Betsy," she asked one day to one of her friends, "do you ever get lonely?" Betsy looked at her strangely and said, "lonely? No, I don't think so," and she continued chewing her cud.

"Bonnie," Millie asked another friend who was chewing on a green apple that a little boy had just handed to her, "do you ever get lonely?"

"Lonely?" repeated Bonnie enjoying her apple very much and letting the juice roll down her chin. "No," said Bonnie. "I don't think so."

"Maybe it's just me," said Millie to herself. She walked over to the fence and the little boy who was still standing there handed a green apple to her, too.

"Thank you," said Millie as she started chewing on the apple. She laid down with the other cows and together they chewed their cud, but Millie still had a feeling of loneliness.

"Something is missing," thought Millie to herself.

The next day she took a long walk around the pasture. Big fluffy white clouds hung low in the bright blue sky. Little flowers were blooming here and there in the pasture grass. Millie bent down and ate one. Suddenly she heard a strange "Meow" sound coming from the fencerow.

"Is someone there?" Millie asked as she looked around.

"Meow," came the sound again, as Millie looked here and there. It was then that she saw a little grey kitten huddled in some tall grass. It was shaking from fright. "Meow," said the kitten once again.

"Little kitten," said Millie as she bent down to look more closely. "Don't be afraid," said Millie. "I won't harm you." The little grey kitten and Millie touched noses and the kitten stopped shaking.

"Come," said Millie. "If you follow me, I'll take care of you and find you some food." Together the kitten and Millie walked slowly to the barn where they found little pools of milk here and there on the floor of the barn. The kitten was happy to lap the milk and when her tummy was full, she looked up at Millie with big starry eyes. "Meow," said the kitten, but this time it was a happy sound rather than a sad one.

"You can be my friend," said Millie to the kitten as the little kitten started to purr.

That night they both huddled up close together to go to sleep.

Millie had found someone to love and wasn't lonely anymore.

~

Rufus, the Black Moshannon Groundhog

"Someday," said Rufus's mother, "you are going to end up in trouble if you don't pay more attention to the things I tell you not to do!"

"Ah, Mom," said Rufus, "don't worry about me! I'll be careful," and with that he hurried over to a grassy patch by some trees.

Rufus lived in a campground of quaint little cottages that had been built a long time ago in Black Moshannon State Park in Pennsylvania. He was born under Cabin No. 1, up on a hill across from the concession stand and overlooking the Black Moshannon River.

He loved living under the cabin and enjoyed all the grass that sprouted up every spring. There were fourteen cabins all in a row, and he liked to go visiting from one to the other. His favorite past-time was watching people. He never tired seeing the different people that came to each cabin all year round, and he got a special thrill if he heard someone yell, "Groundhog!"

Rufus also liked the way little children clapped their hands when they saw him.

Cabin people always left a lot of scraps around the porches and picnic areas. Rufus enjoyed all of those little snacks.

He also loved to have his picture taken and would sit and pose anytime he saw someone with a camera. But one day Rufus nearly met his waterloo. It all happened when he popped out from under the cabin so suddenly that Mrs. Smith screamed and dropped a whole basket of dishes that she was taking up to the camp sink to wash!

"Yeow!" screamed Mrs. Smith when she saw him. Mrs. Smith lived in the city and had never seen a groundhog before. She had been staying in the cabin with her grown children, and this was her first time to stay in a park area. It so happened that Mr. Smith did not like groundhogs at all. When he heard Mrs. Smith scream, he jumped in his car and drove straight to the park office to complain!

When he returned to Cabin No. 1, a park ranger was with him. He pulled a big trap out of the back of his truck, hoping to catch the naughty groundhog.

"Now you've done it," scolded Rufus's mother. "None of us will be safe and now we will have to watch out for the big trap and hope none of us get caught in it!"

"Well, Rufus," said his father, "from now on you will have to get up a little earlier to go out and eat grass, so that no one will see you. Maybe in time the park ranger will remove the trap and we will be safe again."

Rufus hung his head down and felt bad for causing such a stir. From that day on he tried to remember to follow his dad's rules and go out early to eat and he tried hard not to scare people.

But once in awhile, he still popped out to have his picture taken!

~

The Beginning of Fall

Tom heard a loud, shrill, funny call. "What's that? he asked his mom that day.
"A tree frog," his Mother said. "In fall they sing like that." So right away he ran outdoors but couldn't see one anywhere. He went to play,
and found ONE bee was buzzing, and TWO spiders had spun webs.
And also there were THREE mole holes. "Oh, me!" Tom said. "My Dad will have to help." FOUR crickets ran in front of him. And Tom felt sad they ran too fast to catch! FIVE tan grasshoppers leaped high in the air.
Tom asked his Mother for a can to put them in. Then everywhere
white butterflies were dashing in and out of dry weeds. Tom swung with care.
SIX got away. He gave a shout, for he caught one! SEVEN blackbirds flew above the field. Then from the stout old tree EIGHT leaves blew down. Tom knew
that fall was here. While walking by a field where white heath asters grew
Tom picked NINE flowers and reaching down, he plucked a clover, making it TEN!
His mother called. He gave a sigh. Time to go in, and that was when
she gave him some milk and gingerbread men!

~

The Ice Patch Party

"Oh, Look, Mom," exclaimed Sandy Squirrel, "there's an ice patch just perfect for skating!"

Sure enough, a shiny new ice patch had formed right below the big walnut tree in Farmer Brown's back yard.

"Can we go skating, Mom, please?" begged Sandy as she looked down from her perch on a big tree limb.

Just then she smelled a whiff of smoke drifting from the field below the barn where Farmer Brown had lit a big brush pile.

"And look, Mom, Farmer Brown has a brush fire going!" Sandy's mom peered over tree limbs and could see a big pile of brush smoking away. Sandy added, "just maybe we can toast some goodies over the hot coals tonight, too!"

Sandy's mom looked down towards the field where the brush pile was burning.

"Well, now," she said, "having a party is a good idea. It has been such a long cold winter that I am sure everyone is ready for a big party!"

"Can I go around and invite everyone?" asked Sandy, getting more and more excited.

"Why don't you check with our rabbit neighbors and see if they can come, and tell them to bring a dish of grass and bark," said her mom. "I also saw Tom and Tillie Pheasant picking berries around the burning bushes along Farmer Brown's fence row. See if they can come. If everyone can bring something, we will have plenty of snacks."

"Snacks?" asked father squirrel. He was always hungry. He knew exactly when Farmer Brown put new bird seed in the bird feeders every morning, and was into them right away. He also loved the bread that Mrs. Brown put in the junco feeder box on their back deck. "I'll head to Farmer Brown's barn where he keeps the black walnuts stored. I'll bring a batch back and we can roast them tonight," said father squirrel.

That evening the moon rose high over the meadow. The burn pile had burned down. Hot coals glowed red where the fire had burned. All the little creatures gathered around the coals and started toasting their walnuts, berries, seed pods and bark. Among those that had gathered, there were Mr. and Mrs. Pheasant, several rabbit families, the field mice families, a number of squirrel families, and even several deer families from down in the woods.

"What a wonderful party this is," said Sandy Squirrel as she and her friends spent the evening skating on the ice patch while everyone else hovered around the glowing coals of the burn pile.

So in the winter where there are ice patches and/or a burn pile that has burned down, there is sure to be a gathering of little creatures that come out of the woods and down from the trees in celebration of friendship during the last days of winter; and if you hear some wild howling, you can be certain that the coyote family is also enjoying a special evening of togetherness, long after people go to bed for a good night's sleep.

~

The Chicken Coop Disaster

Blackie, Goldie and Copper were three chickens who lived in a coop with a nice fenced in yard on Farmer Brown's farm. Blackie was a plump handsome chicken. She liked puffing out her big fluffy black feathers so everyone would notice her. Goldie was older than the other hens. Her feathers were golden yellow and looked just a little ragged. Once in awhile she would lay a big fat egg.

Copper was the smaller of the three and had feathers the color of burnt copper, something like the color of a teapot you might see at your grandmother's house.

All three hens would take turns laying eggs. One of them laid brown eggs and the rest laid white eggs. Farmer Brown could never tell which one was laying what since all three hens would often crowd into the same nest! Egg laying, it seems, is a secretive business.

Sometimes when you would walk by the coop you could hear the hens gossiping to one another. "Pock, pock, pock," they would say to each other, in their special chicken language. They seemed content and enjoyed pecking around the green grass in their chicken yard.

Farmer Brown brought home a rooster one day to protect them. Roosters work hard in protecting their flock. They chase away any predators such as raccoons or possums. But Henry, the rooster, was not a good rooster. He would chase the chickens around the yard so much that they quit laying eggs as they were all worn out from running away from him!

Finally Farmer Brown took the rooster and found another home for him. That made the hens happy and they could relax once again.

The three hens looked forward to times when Farmer Brown gave them a handful of shelled corn or sunflower seeds. When they saw him coming, they all ran up to greet him.

One year the winter was especially cold, and the hens had a hard time huddling up to each other to keep warm. Farmer Brown kept a light on in the coop to help them stay warm. How happy they were when springtime finally arrived and they could go outside in their yard again.

But springtime brought out other creatures. Creatures such as raccoons, possums, and weasels were hungry after the long cold winter. They especially liked the thought of chicken meat.

One night Farmer Brown forgot to close up the chicken coop like he usually does. That was a disaster. Tuffy Raccoon had been sniffing around and saw the open door. He called one of his friends and they both went into the coop.

The next day when Farmer Brown went to check on the chickens, only Copper was left. There was no sign of Blackie or Goldic. Those hungry creatures from the woods must have carried them off.

Little Cooper stood there looking very lonely. Farmer Brown patted her on the head and told her he was sorry what had happened to her friends. Copper did not feel like eating the kernels of corn he had for her.

Later that day when Copper was standing in the chicken yard, she felt a hugh rush of wind. It was the Great Spirit from the Animal World. "Do not feel sad, little chicken. Your friends have gone on to another world where they are safe," said the Great Spirit. Copper was not sure what that meant, but it made her feel better.

She decided to start eating the kernels of corn that Farmer Brown had given to her.

A few days later Farmer Brown brought home another hen. "Copper," said Farmer Brown, "This is Gladys. She will be your new friend." Copper was happy to have a new friend. She wouldn't be lonely any more. From that day on, Farmer Brown tried hard to remember not to forget to close up the chicken coop at night! The End!

About the Author

A prolific writer, outdoor nature fan and historian, Inge Logenburg Kyler has written stories and poems all her life in between raising a family and working in township government. "I believe we are meant to use the talents that are given to us," she states, and with that, throughout the years, has become a prize winning and widely published poet and author, having written over twenty books as well as writing a column for the Eaton Rapids Flashes newspaper. Along with writing, Inge enjoys doing watercolors, hiking, gardening, being a member of the Poetry Society of Michigan, a docent at the Michigan State Historical Museum and the Woldumar Nature Center as well as involvement with church and other organizations and activities. Having grown up in the Allegheny Mountains of Pennsylvania, she now lives with her husband, little schnauzer, and cat, in an old farm house out in the country in Michigan.

As well as being published widely in many magazines, anthologies, and newspapers, the following are by the Author:

Chapbooks:
The Wind and the Wood
Tecumseh
Down in the Valley
Canis Lupus
Wood Poems
Stepping Stones
Sons and Daughters
Anteanus
To Neah Bay and Back
On to Cancun
This Old Farm
On to Kamcamagus
Settling through America
Passing Through America
When Fireweed Turns to Cotton
Song of the High Country
Michigan Folktales and Ballads
Man in Number Nine
Snoi-tav-resbo/Observations
Red Raspberries in October
Make Me a Blessing
Nicholas and the Golf Course Cat
Crickets are Chirping but No One Can Hear Them
Search for a House
Life With Nicholas
Holt/Delhi Township; An Arcadia
Pictorial History Book

Printed in the United States
By Bookmasters